As his horse closed the gap, Ace saw the rider in front of him turn. It was Luckert!

Looking back, the outlaw emptied his revolver at Ace. Lead whizzed about Ace's head, but riding at a full gallop had spoiled Luckert's aim.

Suddenly, desperately, Luckert brought his horse to a halt and dismounted, reloading furiously.

Ace hauled his horse up and sprang to the ground just as the outlaw clicked the cylinder into place. The two men faced each other, barely twenty yards apart. Both guns came up together.

There was a flash of fire as Ace fired from his hip, then five more as he raised the gun to eye level.

Luckert squeezed out one wild shot, then collapsed like a burst balloon....

THE BOSS OF THE LAZY 9
was originally published by William Morrow and Company, Inc.

Books by Peter Field

The Boss of the Lazy 9
Drive for Devil's River
Gringo Gun
Outlaw Express
Outlaws Three
Powder Valley Plunder
Rustler's Rock
Sagebrush Swindle
Trail to Troublesome

Published by POCKET BOOKS

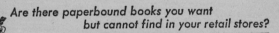 *Are there paperbound books you want
but cannot find in your retail stores?*

You can get any title in print in **POCKET BOOK** editions. Simply send retail price, local sales tax, if any, plus 25¢ to cover mailing and handling costs to:

MAIL SERVICE DEPARTMENT
POCKET BOOKS • A Division of Simon & Schuster, Inc.
1 West 39th Street • New York, New York 10018

Please send check or money order. We cannot be responsible for cash. *Catalogue sent free on request.*

# THE
# BOSS
# OF
# THE
# LAZY
# 9

BY
**PETER FIELD**

PUBLISHED BY POCKET BOOKS NEW YORK

## THE BOSS OF THE LAZY 9

William Morrow edition published 1936

POCKET BOOK edition published March, 1950

2nd printing............June, 1974

L

Standard Book Number: 671-75821-7.

Front cover illustration by John Duillo.

Printed in the U.S.A.

# INTRODUCTION

PETER FIELD was one of the first names I thought of when asked to select outstanding Western novels from the Morrow, Mill and Jefferson House lists for Triple-A Western Classics.

It was in 1934 that Peter Field published his first book. Not many first novels make a reputation for an author. *Outlaws Three* did, and Peter Field's original three characters—lean, shrewd, uncompromising Pat Stevens with his two loyal companions, ugly, implacable Sam Sloan, and huge, dumb Ezra—became famous overnight. And following this trio came many other now famous characters. Peter Field knows his West, and his stories always have plenty of action and suspense, but I have always felt that the primary reason for this author's popularity is that all his characters are right out of life. They have their virtues and their vices. They have their admirable characteristics and their weaknesses. They are like people you know.

In *The Boss of the Lazy 9* you will meet young Ace Gilbert, respected as much for his character as for his straight shooting; Sheriff Dave Robertson, faced not only by a tough rustling problem, but strange stories of an outlaw who did not seem to be as dead as he should have been; the fascinating Ruth Cameron of the great Cameron spread, engaged to young Ace Gilbert; and a group of other characters with whom you will race through as exciting a story as you have read for an age and whom you will remember for a long time.

ERLE STANLEY GARDNER

Temecula, California
September, 1948

# CONTENTS

# 1 • "ACE"

NAMES ARE little more than handles tacked on to human pots and pans for convenience's sake, and yet there are those who make much of them and claim that the names by which a man is known depict the man. Nicknames they mean, of course, since those are the titles a man earns by deeds or by his looks or by the manner of man he is. But even Christian names sometimes have meanings, and sometimes they are strangely apt.

Take Asher Laird Gilbert, for example. His mother named him Asher because the name means, "Lucky; happy"; and those were the gifts she wished for her son. His father named him Laird because, "It's a strong name, and it's Scottish; and what's more, it comes from the manor lords of the old country and they were good, stout men with a love of the land in 'em. That's what I'm wantin' my son to be, too; for it's the land that's the wealth o' the country, Mary. We'll teach him that." The Gilbert was hardly a matter of choice, of course; yet it had a meaning, too. For "Gilbert" means "Golden," according to the old book-legends of names, and Asher Gilbert was gifted with gold by inheritance and with the faculty of making wealth besides.

The Asher became Ash inevitably; and yet there was something peculiarly fitting about it, too. The Ash is a sturdy tree, and a strong one; and its wood is elastic and tough. Ash became "Ace" later on, and the nickname was fitting too. It had to do with cards, for Asher was "lucky" as his mother had wished; and the Ace is the top card of the suit, which was also apt. Asher Laird

Gilbert; Ash, to a few of his friends; Ace to friend and foe alike; Asher to Ruth Cameron, who was to be Ruth Gilbert one day; and Lord Gil to Ruth Cameron's sister, Kay, who was an impertinent minx at best and lacking in proper respect for her elders. . . .

Sheriff Dave Robertson got up from his chair on the porch of the Drovers' Hotel and walked down the four wooden steps to the street, his gaze fixed thoughtfully on the tall white stallion swinging down the street at a springy, tight-muscled lope. The stallion was a magnificent animal, and Dave Robertson had an eye for good horseflesh. But just now his thoughts were less upon the horse than upon the man on the stallion's back. The fact that he had risen and walked down to meet the rider spoke eloquently of his respect for the man. Dave Robertson did not go out of his way to meet any man . . . usually.

"Howdy, Ace." Robertson stood on the plank sidewalk between the Drovers' and the hitching rack, watching the stallion's approach with a subconscious approval. The man in the saddle grinned and nodded a greeting: "Howdy, Dave." The stallion tossed his head proudly and curveted as the rider swung down, and Robertson turned his attention fully on the man.

"Yuh missed the meetin' this afternoon, Ace. Reckon yuh was invited, wasn't yuh?"

Ace Gilbert spoke over his shoulder, carelessly, as he lifted one saddle skirt and loosed the cinch under the stallion's flank. "I was invited, all right, Dave. Reckon you-all didn't miss me much."

"Yuh're wrong, Ace. We did miss yuh." Gilbert had lowered the saddle skirt again and had turned to walk slowly up toward the sidewalk, beating the dust from his chaps with his hat as he walked. Robertson met him at the edge of the walk, choosing the six-inch advantage between ground and curb to bring his own eyes to a level with those of the man he addressed. Ace Gilbert was a tall man, with broad shoulders. Above them his face was lean, with a blue, direct gaze and firm-lipped mouth, the face of a man at peace with his world, but one to fight to the finish if need arose.

Robertson spoke bluntly, his words emphatic, despite the lowness of his voice. "We *need* yuh, Gilbert! We need a leader; and yuh're the man for the job. The *only* man! Plenty o' men are waitin' to see which way yuh jump, Ace. They'd follow yuh where they wouldn't follow another livin' man."

Ace Gilbert grinned slowly. "Reckon you're exaggeratin' some, Dave," he said. "I'm not important to your plans. And if I am . . . well, Dave, I'm sorry for your plans, then. I think you're makin' a mistake. That's why I wasn't at the meetin'."

"Yuh mean yuh're sidin' with Buck Wilbur and the wild bunch!"

Gilbert's smile widened a little. "You know better'n that, Dave," he said gently.

David Robertson frowned a little and dropped his eyes. "Yes, I know better'n that," he admitted grudgingly. "But—yuh can't be neutral, Ace! Dammit, a man like yuh has got t' be for a thing, or against it. Yuh ain't cut out t' be a namby-pamby fence-sitter!"

"No. And I'm not cut out to be a cat's-paw, rakin' other men's chestnuts out of a fire, Dave! When the Lazy 9 starts losin' cattle, you won't find me sittin' on any fence; and you won't find me sittin' in a meetin' yellin' for help, either! I've always made it a practice to kill my own snakes. I wouldn't ask a whole community to turn out and do my dirty work for me, and I don't aim to turn out to do theirs."

"But it's a community matter, Ace!"

"I reckon not. Nobody's stealin' my cows, yet. Nor Hitchcock's, nor any at all on my side of the river. Fact is, most of the rustlin' I've heard about is on the other side of the Divide. Wes Luckert's been makin' a fuss lately about losin' Triangle beef, of course; but the Triangle is big enough to keep its own range clean, I reckon. Far as the boys across the Divide are concerned, let 'em do their own hangin'."

"But the Triangle—Steve Cameron is your neighbor;

him and your dad was close friends. Tubby Martin, and Cal James, and Long—they've lost stock, too, and they're friends of yuhrs."

"Certainly. And I'm engaged to marry Steve Cameron's daughter, Ruth. If, and when, Steve Cameron asks me for help against rustlers or anything else, the Lazy 9 will ride hell-for-leather! Same thing goes for the others you named. Right now, Steve Cameron is more interested in gettin' himself re-elected Speaker of the House up at Salt Lake than he is in any two-bit rustlers down here on Thunder River. I figure Luckert has let himself get stampeded because he's lost a few cows and knows he's apt to be first to suffer if rustlin' gets really bad—his range bein' closest to the hills. The others aren't losin' many yet, are they?"

"You can't wait till they start drivin' off whole herds, Ace! Once outlawry gets a start on a range, it's harder to kill out than jimson grass."

Gilbert smiled a little. "This meetin' of yours, Dave: The idea was to organize vigilantes, wasn't it?"

"We organized 'em, too! Jim Talbert's leader. But—he'd step down gladly if yuh'd take his place, Ace. Yuh're the man . . ."

"Talbert, eh? I'm sorry you picked on Jim. He's a newcomer, and this'll make him the target for the bad ones, and the butt for the rest of you if he makes mistakes. . . . But, speakin' of outlawry, Dave; you reckon these vigilantes aim to stay strictly inside the law?"

"They aim to hang rustlers when caught, Ace. Yuh know that! It takes strong medicine to scotch this kind of snake, and if it's strong enough yuh need fewer doses!"

But Gilbert shook his head. "Sorry, Dave, but I'm not takin' any. Catch your rustler—if you can; string him up, and what've you done? You've killed a man—likely a poor wrong-headed underdog that was doin' somebody else's dirty work same as your vigilantes are doin' —and the big fellow goes free. Understand me, if I catch rustlers on my range I won't exactly coddle 'em! But there's more behind this business of rustlin', and meetin's, and what-not, than meets the eye. I don't know what it is—yet. Somebody's grindin' an axe, and all we're seein' right now is the sparks. I aim to wait till I see who's turnin' the grindstone."

Robertson shrugged. "No use arguin' with yuh, Ace; I know that. If that's the way yuh've set your mind, I reckon I can't change it for yuh. But I'm warnin' yuh, yuh're stayin' neutral like this is goin' to be misunderstood—plenty!"

"I can stand that." Ace shifted his weight easily to the other foot, put his hat on the back of his head, and changed the subject with a grin at Robertson. "You think the market'll hold up through shippin' time? Beef's bringin' better prices now than it has since I can remember."

"Yeah," said Robertson, and sighed. "That's how-come so much rustlin'. Likely prices'll drop some when shippin' starts; but I reckon we'll still get a good figure." He looked at Ace and grinned, as if to say 'my turn now at changin' the subject,' and asked slyly: "When's Miss Ruth comin' home, Ace? She's been gone most a year now, ain't she? Looks like she could see a lot of Europe in that time."

"She got in this afternoon, Dave. Hadn't you heard?" Ace Gilbert's smile had a deeper quality now than it had had before. "That's why I'm in town. She was tired after her trip, so I left her at Ma Watson's for tonight. She'll go on out to the Triangle tomorrow. It's only been eleven months, really, since she left; but it seems longer to me!" He laughed a little, half-ashamed of the emphasis his words had held. "I'm in for a game with the boys tonight—I aim to be busy, evenin's, for a while, you see! Have a drink with me to start the evenin'?"

"No, thanks, Ace. Just had supper, and I got t' humor my stomach these days. I'll set a while; drop in later and see how much yuh lost!"

He returned slowly to his seat on the porch and Ace Gilbert turned for a farewell word with his horse before crossing the street toward the Palace Bar. The stallion's ears went back and the lean, wickedly beautiful head struck down, teeth bared, at Gilbert's arm. The gleaming teeth snapped shut just safely clear of flesh and the white horse nibbled gently at the cloth of the man's shirt sleeve, jerking it a little. The man laughed, deep in his throat, and took the big head in his arms. The stallion's ears came forward one at a time, and he whinnied softly with a sound that matched the man's laughter. "Bite me, would you?" Gilbert cuffed the small ears back and gripped the horse's jaw in his two hands, shaking him as one might a dog. "Bite me, would you? Bad horse, are you? Why, damn you, Satan, I'll . . ." But the stallion butted him gently and jarred the threat out of him, and Gilbert laughed again. Passing the stallion, then, the man's hand dropped caressingly on the horse's rump and dragged down, fingers combing the long white tail and dragging it out behind him. It was as if the man were loath to lose his touch on the horse; and Satan, turning his head far back, whinnied softly through his nose in farewell.

Dave Robertson, watching from the Drovers' porch, found a smile on his lips as Ace Gilbert crossed the street. He erased the smile as he felt the eyes of his neighbor upon him, and then grinned frankly. "Sort o' nice t' see a man and horse lovin' each other like them two do," he said. "That's a damn fine horse, too, that Satan. Nothin' in Utah that's better!"

"Yeah. And I reckon yuh'd take in more territory'n that 'fore yuh'd find a better man than the one that tops him, too! Jim Talbert's a good man, and all; but if yuh fellers really aim t' clean up this here, now, range it 'pears t' me like yuh made a mistake not pickin' Ace t' lead yuh. Eh?"

Robertson shot one glowering glance at the hotel clerk who had dared point out the particular weakness that was worrying Robertson himself the most, and then took refuge once more in dignified silence. There was such a thing as rubbing it in!

## 2 • "WES"

As ACE came up to the door of the Palace Bar, a man came out and stood watching him from the sill. A big man, with a black spade beard that jutted out from below his chin, his eyes hidden in the deep shadow cast by his hat.

"Why—hello, Talbert," said Ace. "Just been hearing how you're going to head the vigilantes. I'm glad the boys put up so good a man." He would have passed on then, into the bar. For after all, he knew Talbert very little. The man had not been in Wells very long, and Ace had had little contact with him. His greeting had been one of politeness, that was all. But Talbert stopped him with a gesture.

"Why, I reckon they would rather have had you, Gilbert," he said, and smiled, a half-apologetic smile. "But seein' as they've elected me, I'll do my best." Ace nodded, and once more made for the door. But Talbert was speaking again.

"You've been in this country longer than I have, Gilbert—I'd like to know what you think of this situation. Got any ideas on where the rustlers are coming from?" Ace had been watching the spade beard, as if fascinated by the way it wiggled as the man's mouth moved. Now his gaze moved up to Talbert's eyes—or rather, to the deep band of shadow in which the eyes were scarcely visible. He was surprised, and a little taken aback. Talbert's voice was ingratiating, almost a little anxious. "Tough on him," thought Ace. "New country to him, he's hardly settled, and being thrown into the thick of things this way."

7

"Why no, Talbert," he answered courteously, "can't say as I have. Of course, I haven't missed any stock from the Lazy 9 yet, so I haven't had to do much thinking, nor had a chance to see how the rustlers are working."

"I see," said Talbert, and something in his voice made Ace look more sharply at that band of shadow, trying to pierce through it to the hidden eyes. "Well, I won't keep you any longer," said Talbert, and moved down the steps. Ace watched him walk slowly along the street. He was puzzled. Why the change in Talbert's attitude? He had been pleasant enough before, and then suddenly his voice had chilled, faintly, but perceptibly. Ace watched him until he had turned into the livery stable down the street, then, shrugging his shoulders, he pushed his way through the door of the Palace Bar.

A dozen men called his name in greeting as he entered, and the line at the bar shoved aside to make room for him. He paused in the doorway briefly, lifting his white hat high in salute. "Howdy, Boys! Howdy, Ed! Charley! 'Lo, Nick! Who's thirsty? Make mine Bourbon, Joe; and how's the wife and kids?"

"Hi, Ace, yuh ol' hoss-thief!" A clear, high voice rang out from a poker table at the rear of the room and Gilbert turned that way, smiling. "Come on and set in, durn yuh! I'm still raw from the hidin' yuh give me last time yuh was in town, and I'm thirstin' for revenge!"

"Shucks, Cal, you wouldn't hold a streak of luck against a man, would you? You boys play too fast a game for me, anyway. Me bein' just a learner . . ."

"Learner, hell!" A new voice cut in, also from the poker table, and the honest sadness in the tone won a roar of laughter. Gilbert downed a drink at the bar and walked back to join the group at the table, answering a series of friendly greetings on the way.

"Well, I'll set in," he said. "If you boys don't mind holdin' up the game now and then to explain things to me. Two pair, now, that beats four of a kind, don't it? And a flush beats a full house. . . ."

"Yeah, and with two tens and a five yuh can meld fifteen-two, fifteen-four and six for a pair not to mention high, low, jack and game! Set down, yuh false alarm, and shuffle the cyards! Yuh're jest in time t' deal!" Tommy Hitchcock's tone was mildly sarcastic.

"Thanks, Tommy! Never can keep those things straight in my head. . . . Why, howdy, Wes. How's thing's goin' on the Triangle?"

The big man at the end of the table grunted a surly answer. The foreman of the Triangle was a dark, powerfully built man, quick in his movements like a mountain cat. His face was surly now, the brow drawn to a thick crease between his narrow eyes. Gilbert picked up the cards as he slid into the empty seat. He shuffled the pack, grinning at the circle of faces around the board.

"Now, gents, if nobody's got any other ideas, we'll play *honest* poker for a while! All set? Here they come."

Wes Luckert, opposite Ace, glanced up, scowling. "Ain't insinuatin' that we been playin' any *other* kind o' poker, are yuh, Gilbert?" he said.

"Not insinuatin', Wes." There had been unmasked bitterness in the man's tone, but Gilbert's answering voice was unruffled and cool. "Just statin' a fact! You wasn't supposin' the game was honest, were you? Not with Cal James, and Tommy Hitchcock, and Lyle Long, and Tubby Martin in it? Lord, Wes, you must be an optimist!" His grin took the sting out of the words and he met Luckert's black look laughingly. "Anyway, I hadn't noticed before that *you* were the big winner, Wes," he added thoughtfully.

Luckert's answering growl was lost in the shout of laughter that went up at his expense, and the game moved on. Within a dozen hands, Ace Gilbert had doubled his stack of chips before him on the table and Tubby Martin made mournful comment.

"Lucky at cards, unlucky at love is what they say," he remarked plaintively. "Is that how-come yuh're with us tonight, Ace? I thought Miss Ruth got home today?"

"She did. But she was tired from the trip, so I left her at Ma Watson's to catch some sleep. You boys better get your revenge tonight, I warn you! I aim to be right busy in better company o' nights, after this!"

Wes Luckert laughed shortly. "Yeah? Well, maybe so; but nobody'd ever figger from the *passionate* welcome yuh got at the station this evenin' that Ruth aimed t' monopolize yuhr time, Gilbert!"

Ace Gilbert flushed a little beneath his tan. That scene at the station when Ruth Cameron stepped down from her train into the arms of her fiancé had failed, somehow, to come up to the mark of his own anticipations; had failed to satisfy the lonely hunger of the long months of her absence. Luckert's taunt brought the details of the meeting back with vivid freshness: The crowd of Triangle riders led by Luckert, come to welcome their employer's daughter—the moments of waiting; breathless, eager moments for Ace—the first glimpse of the girl in the Pullman door, tall and poised and a little aloof from the boisterous crowd beneath—the brief, tense moment when he had taken her in his arms and sought her lips, finding them cool and firm and unyielding, her body rigid and resentful of his embrace, her low-voiced protest as she put him off:

"Please, Asher! Don't maul me! . . . Of course I'm glad to see you, dear; but—after all, we aren't alone! . . . Hello, boys. Nice of you all to come. You brought a mount for me, Wes? Thanks. I'll stay in town tonight, I think, and ride out tomorrow. Asher, see about my bags, do you mind?"

The men at the table now sensed Gilbert's hurt and busied themselves with the cards, faces averted from his discomfiture. Cal James cut the deck and Lyle Long flipped the down cards around with an effort at gayety. "Come on, pasteboards!" he chanted. "Bring that money home! Poker's goin' up from now on, friends! I aim to bar all grocery clerks . . ."

But Gilbert's voice cut through the lesser talk. "It all depends on the kind of girls a man's used to, I reckon, Wes," he said quietly. An innocent remark, seemingly; innocently said, certainly. But Tubby Martin choked suddenly and his face turned very red; and Tommy Hitchcock was seized all at once with a fit of coughing. Wes Luckert, in the past few months, had turned squire to a flame-haired belle in a dance hall further down the street and it was common knowledge that that lady's temperament, at least, took no heed of crowds in the airing of her moods, sentimental or otherwise. The fact had been proved more than once, and to the painful embarrassment of the Triangle foreman, too.

Luckert's face darkened swiftly and he pushed his chair back as if to rise. "Not gettin' personal, are yuh, Gilbert?" he growled.

Gilbert's brows lifted a bit, innocently. "Why, of course not, Wes. Just a generality, that's all. . . . Applies to me as much as anyone, I reckon, judgin' by the mistake I made today. By the way, Lyle, were you at the meetin' this afternoon?" He switched the subject deftly, having won his point. "Understand things are goin' to be done about the rustlin' that's been goin' on."

Long shrugged. "I was there," he said. "If yuh understand anything at all about what was done, though, yuh got me beat! All I heard was a lot o' talk about constitutional rights and the spotless honor o' the sovereign state o' Utah! Noticed that the Lazy 9 wasn't represented, though. Wasn't the only one that noticed it, either."

Luckert's heavier voice cut in again. "Reckon Gilbert would've felt right queer in a meetin' like that. Somebody might've called to him t' explain how come he ain't lost no beef."

Ace favored the Triangle foreman with a slantwise glance. "Meanin'?" he said, softly.

Luckert laughed. "Reckon it ain't hard t' figger what I mean," he said. "It looks sort o' queer when one outfit stands out against enforcin' the law, especially when that outfit's the one that ain't been hit by the wild bunch! Looks like that party might be afraid t' have things looked into, don't it?"

Ace's mind flashed back to Talbert's cool "I see" of a few moments before, and his eyes narrowed. Evidently Luckert had been talking this way before and to other people. That explained the change in the bearded man's attitude, then. He turned to Luckert and laughed softly. . . . "I was waitin' for you to put it into words, Wes," he said. "I've been hearin' rumors for quite a while. . . . You ought to know better than to try to ride me, Wes. Here's where it stops!" His voice changed suddenly, turning hard and sharp. "Put up or shut up, Luckert! I'm callin' your bluff!"

Gilbert stood up slowly, stepping clear of his chair. Wes Luckert lunged to his feet, the thrust of his knees sending his chair backward with a crash. His right hand whipped back as he straightened, tugging at his holstered gun; but Tommy Hitchcock, at Luckert's right, was quicker. He flung forward, both hands clutching at Luckert's wrist; dropped his entire weight on Luckert's arm, holding the gun down inside its sheath.

"Don't do that, Luckert, yuh damn fool!" he growled harshly. "Yuh want t' get killed?"

Across the table, Ace Gilbert's lips twisted a little in a half-smile and the poised alertness of his pose relaxed a bit. "Take off the gun, Wes," he said. "We'll settle this another way!" His own hands dropped to the buckle that held the gun-belt at his hip, and he tossed weapon and harness into Tubby Martin's lap.

Martin looked up, his round face solemn and worried, as Luckert ripped his own gun free and gave it up. "He's got twenty pounds on yuh, Ace. Yuh sure yuh know what yuh're doin', boy?"

Gilbert's smile remained unchanged. "He's askin' for it, Tubby," he said gently. "I'd rather risk a lickin' than have to kill him!"

# 3 · "NEXT TIME"

LUCKERT FLUNG out one hairy paw and hurled a chair aside, leaving a cleared space of a dozen feet between himself and Ace. The crowd in the big room surged in about the two poised men, forming a tight, eager circle. Luckert tossed the hair back from his face and stooped forward a little, his heavy arms hanging loose. His lips were pulled back in an ugly smile.

"Guns or bare hands, Gilbert—all the same t' me! I'll kill yuh, yuh two-faced, lyin' cow-thief! It'll take longer this way, that's all!"

Gilbert's low-toned answer was a red rag flung in the face of a bull. "You talk too much for a fightin' man, Wes," he said.

And Luckert charged. There was no pretty fencing for an opening in the man's attack; no attempt to shield himself. It was the berserk lunge of a maddened man, hungry for the feel of flesh against his hands, seeking to crush or maul.

Ace Gilbert whipped both hands upward in slashing hooks to Luckert's face as the big man came in, but they were not enough to stop the momentum of the charge. Luckert's head struck low in Gilbert's chest and the two reeled back together, bringing up with crushing force against the mass of bodies that hemmed them in. Gilbert's hands were blocked for a moment by the weight of Luckert's body and in that instant while they stood locked against the crowd Wes Luckert's knee ripped up and barely missed the groin, driving deep into Gilbert's waist. The pain of it drained the color from Gilbert's face and left him weak. As Luckert stepped back a lit-

13

tle, Ace barely found strength to lift his hands; but not in time to block the flailing blow that found his unprotected jaw. He spun before that punishing fist, twisting along the tight-pressed bodies of the crowd to fall sidelong and twist face down along the floor.

Luckert laughed then, triumphantly; and it was that instant of pause that spoiled his victory. Gilbert lifted his body on his hands, staring down at the crimson flecks that marked the floor. Blood; his own. He twisted, glimpsing the blur of booted feet as Luckert came in to clinch his triumph. One single boot struck out from the blur of legs that danced in Gilbert's eyes, and he felt it strike heavily against his side. He doubled his body around it, swinging upward and back with all the strength of his back. His hands encountered the rowel of Luckert's spur and the sting of it made him laugh. Better there than in the face, where Luckert would have driven it in another minute! And the thought lent added fury to the surging heave that lifted Luckert off his feet and spun him back across the circle to the floor.

The big man's head struck with blinding force at the feet of the spectators across the ring and he lay still for the moment, breathing heavily. Gilbert stood inert, swaying a little, sucking in the breath that fed his returning strength. A hand clutched at his arm and he heard a voice behind him which he recognized as Long's; but he could not make out the words. The haze was fading from before his eyes now, and his head seemed clear. Luckert was getting up at last, drawing himself together and lifting his hulking body to a stand. His face was smeared with red and the sight of it brought a twisted grin to Gilbert's face. Those first whipping hooks as Luckert came in had told a little, anyway!

Ace waited until Luckert stood erect. Each tiny second brought back new strength and he would need it all. Delay helped Luckert, too; but that could not be helped. Luckert shook his head fiercely, clearing his sight. His hands came up uncertainly . . . and it was then that Gilbert charged.

He flung his weight forward from his toes as a diver

takes the whip of a board; shot forward, straight and low and flashed both hands in a swift one-two just under Luckert's ribs. The impact stopped his charge and he felt Luckert double at the waist, grunting. Ace straightened then, whipping his right hand up through Luckert's crumbling guard; felt it meet the big man's jaw with a jar that shot a stream of pain back through the wrist and up the whole forearm.

Luckert sagged backward, driven back upon his heels against the solid wall of men that held him in. He rested there a moment, groggily. As he straightened, Gilbert's left shot in again and drove him back. He mouthed an oath, drooling blood from mangled lips. Gilbert's right was numbed, but he hooked it up again, fascinated by the jerk of Luckert's head as the blows smashed home. Another left; a right; Luckert's face was horrid now, and his flailing arms were little more than clubs, swung aimlessly and without effect. The crowd was yelling, and Ace heard separate words for the first time since the fight began. Tubby Martin—fat, friendly man—was howling two short words, repeated endlessly: "Kill him! Kill him!" Someone somewhere was screaming joyous oaths. Another voice: "The jaw, Ace! Never mind his face! The button, hit him on the button!"

"Oh, all right!" Ace wondered if he spoke the words aloud. "The jaw, then!" Crack! . . . Damn! The right wasn't so numb, after all! Hurt clear to the shoulder, that time. Maybe a bone was gone. . . . But Luckert was going down! Ace dropped his hands slowly, staring at the crumpling hulk sinking slowly down against the wall of men that had delayed his fall. Luckert was down! Ace stepped back, wiping his hands against his shirt where they left bloody stains. Hands gripped him from every side and a score of voices rang in his ears. He made out one face that he recognized—Cal James. There was Hitchcock, too; and Martin. Tubby had stopped saying "Kill him!" Had stopped saying anything, in fact; anything articulate, at least.

"Thanks, Tommy, for stoppin' his draw," he said. "I —I'm glad I didn't have to—kill him."

Hitchcock laughed. "If yuh ever get sore at me, Ace, yuh shoot me!" he said. "I'd like that better than what yuh gave Luckert!"

"I took some, too." Ace felt his jaw ruefully. "Do I look bad, Cal?"

"Yuh look like hell, son, but yuh'll wash! Luckert won't! Soap and water won't have much effect on him! Nothin' but time'll mend *his* looks! Yuh come with me and I'll fix yuh up. Hey, Joe! Get some hot water back t' yuhr private room pronto, yuh hear? Come on, Ace. I want a talk with yuh, anyway."

They made their way back through the crowd to the tiny room which served the bartender as a home. Joe was there with a pan of water which he put to heat on the tiny stove before he left the two men alone. Ace stripped to the waist and submitted to Cal James' care. Through the medium of a cracked mirror he watched the restoration of his face, finding the damage somewhat less than he had feared. His lip was cut a little and there was an angry bruise along his jaw. Other bruises showed against the clear white of his body where Luckert's boot and random blows had struck, but they would at least be hidden to ache unseen!

"It's too bad Tommy didn't let him make his draw." Cal James spoke at last, thoughtfully. "Yuh'd be better off if yuh'd killed him, Ace. Yuh'll have t' do it some day, and this was a chance t' make it a square shoot-out before witnesses. He wouldn't risk that unless he was crazy mad like he was tonight. Next time, he'll ambush yuh, or else hire it done."

Gilbert laughed deprecatingly. "I reckon you're seein' things, Cal," he said. "I been hearin' rumors, too, of course; but Luckert hasn't any fight with me, really. He's just got a burr in him somewhere and it's makin' him pitch."

"Maybe. . . . How long's it been since yuh was at the Triangle?"

"Some time. Ruth's been gone, yuh know; and the Colonel's been playin' politics. None of the family there, now. Even Kay's been gone all winter; in some girl's school in 'Frisco, she is. Why?"

"I dropped in, casual-like, day before yesterday. Luckert's been hirin' men, Ace. Not ordinary cow-hands, either. Bad hombres! Every other man on the Triangle now talks with a Texas drawl!"

Ace chuckled. "Nothin' against a man because he slurs his r's, is it, Cal?"

"All right, laugh if yuh want! I'm older'n yuh are, son; and I've seen some things. These new hombres at the Triangle are gun-slingers; Texas warriors; the kind that sells their guns t' the best bidder! I've seen trouble start on other ranges, and I know the breed! There's a range war breedin' on Thunder River as sure as I'm a foot high, Ace; and Wes Luckert is behind it, somehow! Now, you tell me—*why?*"

"That's it. That's where your story falls down, Cal. There isn't any reason! Wes Luckert and I have never been friends; just never cottoned to each other. We've had a dozen little run-in's like the one today, only it always ended short of a fight, before. Lately, this rustlin' business has been gettin' on Wes's nerves and he's been talkin' too much. Naturally, dislikin' me the way he does, he's sort of hopin' it'll turn out that I've got somethin' to do with the rustlin' and his mind's been runnin' that way. I called him today just because it wouldn't do to let talk like that go too far. With folks stirred up the way they are now, a rumor can get right serious if it's let to run. But Wes Luckert's got no reason for wantin' me killed! And he's got no reason for startin' a range war."

Cal James shrugged, still unconvinced. "Maybe yuh're right; maybe not. I know gun-slingers when I see 'em, though. And the Triangle's lousy with 'em!"

"Maybe Wes is importin' men for the vigilantes. I hear he's the main one that's howlin' about losin' beef."

"That's a funny thing, too." Cal James pounced upon the suggestion avidly. "Yuh're right about Wes yelpin' over losin' Triangle beef; but he didn't start complainin' until the talk about organizin' the vigilantes was already

begun! Tubby Martin and Long have both been losin'
heavy, too. Their ranges both border on the hills, same
as the Triangle does. So does Jim Talbert's Rockin' M
spread; and he's been losin' beef, same as the others. I
reckon Wes heard *them* talk about losin' cows so he
thought it was up t' *him* t' howl, too!"

But Ace only laughed. "Shucks, Cal! You don't like
Luckert and you're determined to see somethin' spooky
about him! Come to, man, and stop seeing ghosts! Wes
has no reason to hate me. Hand me my shirt now and
let's get back outside. Boys'll be thinkin' you had to per-
form a major operation on me, or somethin'!"

They returned to the outer room to become part of
a talkative, congratulatory crowd that gathered at once
about Gilbert. Luckert had been taken away to some
other place and the crowd in the Palace was a Gilbert
crowd; but the evening had lost its flavor for Ace and
he broke away early to seek his room in the Drovers'
Hotel.

The day had been one of mingled emotions; the poign-
ant pleasure of Ruth Cameron's return mixed with the
lingering hurt of her coolness, and later the mad, fierce
joy of battle mixed with a guilty inner knowledge that
he had fought under false colors.

"It was because he sneered at the way Ruth took my
kiss that I fought him," he told himself, frankly. "I could
have dodged the other thing. Nobody'd have believed
it anyway. But he hit a sore spot with his first shot,
and I jumped at the first chance to get even without
havin' it said we fought over Ruth. . . . She *was* cold
to me; but then, I ought to know by now that that's
her way. She's proud as the devil, and—I guess I was
pretty crude, pawin' at her that way. I reckon I'd missed
her too much; got to lookin' forward to her comin' home
so hard I never stopped to think that she wouldn't be
feelin' the way I did. I should've known she couldn't
stop bein'—dignified!" He laughed a little. "And I
wouldn't want her to, either," he added, loyally. It did
not occur to him that his loyalty was a little belated;

that it was an afterthought. He would have denied it fiercely had he been so accused.

He glanced at his battered face in the glass above the wash-stand. Ruth would question him about that tomorrow; would certainly not approve of a public brawl. The fact that he had fought her father's own foreman would hardly lessen her disapproval, either, he thought. Well, he regretted it himself. The Camerons and the Gilberts had been friends and neighbors for thirty years. Dave Cameron's Triangle, north of Thunder River and skirting the Mescalero hills, and Gilbert's Lazy 9, south of the river, had the distinction of being the largest cattle spreads in the valley. Andrew Gilbert and Dave Cameron had registered their brands in the same year and had been the best of friends. When the Lazy 9 descended to Asher Gilbert at the death of his father, the friendship had continued and bade fair to assume even closer ties, for young Asher had become the favored swain of Ruth Cameron, Dave Cameron's eldest daughter. Both spreads had prospered throughout the years, and with prosperity had come for Dave Cameron the opportunity to gratify his life's ambition in politics. He was "Colonel" Cameron now; member of the State Senate, and a prominent figure in the political business of the northwest. Outside interests had drawn the Camerons away from their home on the Thunder River range and the Triangle had gone on under the guidance of other men. Wes Luckert was the last of these; an able cowman who had risen in two years' time from common puncher, newly hired, to boss of the Triangle range.

Ruth Cameron, the summer following her graduation from a west coast university, had succumbed at last to Asher Gilbert's wooing and had promised to be his wife, stipulating only that the date be set a year in advance to allow her time for the European trip that was her father's graduation gift. Gilbert had been too proud of his success to quarrel over terms and the girl had spent ten full months abroad; months in the course of which Ace Gilbert realized the full price of his concession in loneliness.

Ruth's sister, Kathryn, three years her junior, had been absent, too, at a private school on the coast; so that the Triangle ranch house had offered no solace at all to the deserted swain. Not that Kay Cameron could have solaced his loneliness for Ruth in any event, of course. Kay was hardly more than a child, and something of a tomboy to boot; a nice enough child, of course, but utterly unlike her regal sister.

As if designedly to take advantage of Dave Cameron's absence, the range had suffered in the past year from a plague of rustling that had caused no little complaint from the ranchers nearest the Mescalero hills. The Lazy 9, south of the river and distant from the hills, had suffered only its usual small percent of loss; but the Triangle at least was being really hurt. From that fact alone the conclusion was obvious: rustlers had made headquarters in the hills and were preying on the nearer ranges, first on the northern side of the mountains and now in the Thunder River valley as well. No one but Wes Luckert even pretended any other explanation as plausible; but recently there had been drifting rumors, reaching Gilbert naturally in due course, of remarks by Luckert to the effect that the missing beef might not have gone north at all, but south across the river onto Lazy 9 range. Ace had paid no attention to the rumors, had forgotten them, in fact; even Talbert's curious change of tone had not recalled them to him, until Wes's sneer at the poker table. Tonight's battle in the Palace had been the outgrowth of those rumors; or at least that would be the public explanation of the fight. Ace Gilbert's own admission as to its cause would never go beyond himself!

He awakened with the sun the next morning and turned his back to the window, courting sleep as a killer of time. Ruth would not be up for hours yet, he guessed, and the morning would be empty. But sleep would not return and he arose at last and ate breakfast in an empty dining room. Martin and Hitchcock and James and Long had already eaten, he learned from the waitress, each one having risen early to return to his ranch. The

Palace Bar was empty, too, except for its proprietor, the paunchy man whose only known title was Joe. The place smelled of stale smoke and beer and its untidy tables and scattered chairs had the look of a blowsy wench caught after dawn in tawdry spangles.

Joe grunted a sleepy greeting and offered whiskey. Gilbert refused the drink, making a face at the smell of it. Joe shrugged and flapped a sodden cloth at the bar.

"Feller in here 'while ago said there's a registered package for yuh down at the station. Said the agent wouldn't let him bring it 'cause yuh have t' sign fer it."

Ace thanked him. That would provide a means of filling the time before he would see Ruth, at any rate. The station bearing the name of Buffalo Wells was four miles south of the town proper. The package would probably be some mail-order purchase made by one of the Lazy 9 riders and sent in Gilbert's name in the likely event that the buyer should be broke when the purchase arrived. He could sign for it, and if it proved too bulky for carrying it could come later on the stage.

He saddled the white stallion in the box stall in which it had been left for the night and rode southward in a brighter mood. The trip would kill an hour or so, and when he returned it would be time to call for Ruth. Her blooded sorrel, brought in yesterday by the Triangle men, had been left at her orders in the livery barn and she would ride home with Ace today. It occurred to him that they might have a lunch put up in town and eat together on the way. It would be nice to prolong as much as possible their first time alone together since her return.

The station was a box-like structure of two stories which provided both office and living quarters for the wizened, sour little man placed in charge by the railroad. It was flanked on the east by a water tower, standing high on its four spraddling legs like some giant, obese bug; and on the east by a maze of whitewashed fences that formed the shipping pens. There was a tool house across the tracks, windowless and unpainted. The place seemed entirely dead as Satan's hoof-beats echoed against the weathered wall; deserted and empty. Strange that this should be the link that connected the Thunder River range with life; the connection with the outer world of commerce that had brought prosperity to the land. It gave no hint, certainly, of the throbbing forces of which it was the tangible sign.

Ace dismounted beside the hitching rack at the eastern end of the cinder platform and his boot-heels crunched loudly in the silence as he crossed to the door of the station. The tiny waiting room was empty, naturally; and as Gilbert reached the door the metallic click of the telegraph key inside the office rang loudly in an insistent monotone. Ace crossed to the small, grilled window and glanced in at the deserted desk. The clock facing the ticket grill said eight o'clock. He tapped loudly on the shelf under the grill and waited. The stairs to the upper rooms opened from the inner office so that there was no access from the waiting room; but there was no sound from above to give a hint of occupancy. Ace returned to the door and walked aimlessly down the platform toward the west. Number 7, eastbound, was due at 8:16 and it carried mail. The agent would necessarily be on hand to meet it, so he could not be far away.

A tiny sound reached Gilbert's ear faintly and something clicked in his brain—there was a horse hidden behind the station. The sound he had heard was the jingle of bit-rings. The back of Ace's neck tingled oddly with that queer, unnamed sense that *feels* a steady gaze. Someone was spying on him from the eastern end of the station. Ace knew that as surely as he knew his name. The awareness of danger was as real as the cold breath that comes from an opening door in the dark. And it could mean one thing, only. Cal James' warning came back to him with startling clarity. "Next time he'll ambush yuh, or hire it done!" This was "next time"!

"I'm a fool!" Ace stopped walking and stood staring down the track to the east, from which Number 7 would be coming soon. "Took the bait like a sucker and rode into a trap! Should've known somethin' was wrong when I found the station empty." His mind was running with lightning speed, each impression clear-cut and sharp. "He must've got here just before I topped the ridge, comin' down. Didn't have time to get set. He's waitin' now for me to face him. No witnesses, and if I'm drilled from the front he can claim it was an even break, if he's caught. That means he's usin' a Colt, not a rifle. We're even there, anyway."

He whirled, whipping his gun up in a draw that was lightning fast. A six-gun showed at the eastern corner of the station, and above it, a hat brim and half a man's face. Gilbert's shot ripped splinters from the planking scant inches from the face and the other's shot was wild. Ace leaped sideways then, clearing the tracks alongside the platform and sprawling in the cinders beyond the rails. Lead spanged spitefully against the steel beside him and plowed a dusty furrow past his face. There was a three-foot grade below the roadbed here and Ace struck it in a twisting fall that sent his body down below the tracks.

"Three shots," he murmured, counting instinctively. "Two comin'; maybe three. . . . Unless he's got a second gun! . . . Damn! That gravel didn't improve my looks none! Ruth won't like it. . . . But it's better than what that hombre meant for me, anyway! I wonder what's he doin' now?"

## 4 · KAY

No sound came from the other side of the tracks and Ace pulled his feet under him and ran, crouching, along the embankment to the east. Twenty steps brought him back, even with the eastern end of the station and he stopped there, hugging the grade and bringing his head as high as he dared to peep over the rails. He could not see the platform itself, since his angle of vision slanted upward; but he could see Satan at the hitching rack, and the horse was watching, prick-eared, some object of interest low down along the station wall. Ace grinned. "Layin' low," he guessed. "Keepin' down low and close to the wall, waitin' for me to show."

The rail close to Gilbert's ear was humming now and he knew that Number 7 would be on time. Within a minute or two it would come into sight over the ridge to the east. The man on the other side of the tracks must know that, too. He would make his final play soon, or give up the attempt.

Ace searched the roadbed about him until he found a piece of cinder the size of his fist. He balanced it in his hand, testing its weight; crouched low and turned a little to face the window behind which the telegraph key was clicking again. His right arm went back slowly, bearing the cinder; whipped over in a short arc.

The missile carried true and Ace heard the crash of broken glass. He stood erect then, the Colt leaping from his left hand to his right as he straightened up. A man squatted beside the end wall of the station, a gun poised in his hand. He had glanced aside instinctively as the window smashed—was jerking back now, facing Ace.

The two guns spat a swift one-two, their tongues of flame licking out to cross like red-hot blades. Something tugged sharply at the cloth of Gilbert's shirt just under his raised left arm. The man by the station wall lost his balance and fell back against the house, his feet shooting out from beneath him as he lost his stance. Ace climbed the embankment slowly, his gun held warily on the seated man. There was a spreading stain on the fellow's shirt and his face was ashen. His gun lay smoking in the dust beside him, the butt still held in his loosening grasp. Eastward, a clot of smoke topped the skyline and Number 7 whistled hoarsely as it topped the ridge.

"Fast work," Ace said slowly. "I figured the window breakin' would give me more time."

"Yuh're some sudden yo'self," said the man by the

wall. "That first shot, as yuh turned, nicked my shoulder."

"I never saw you before did I?" Ace's tone was faintly puzzled.

"Nor since." The man's answer was whimsical.

"What made you lay for me?"

The man grinned. "Never did like a man that rode a white hoss," he said.

"Luckert hired you," Ace accused, bluntly.

"Interestin', if true." The other was still grinning. "Who's Luckert?"

"Satan's a good horse," Ace told him, irrelevantly. "How bad are you hurt?"

"I'll die," the stranger opined cheerfully. "How are you?"

Number 7 screamed again, the rapid beat of her exhaust slowing as she neared the stop. Ace Gilbert stooped beside the wounded man and removed the gun from his hand. He holstered his own gun, walking quickly to the door of the station, still ajar since his exit less than five minutes ago. He used the butt of the stranger's gun to drive the hinge-pins from their sockets and carried the door back with him. He laid it down beside the stranger.

"No doctor in Wells fit to tend you," he said. "That's a lung wound, and you'll need good care. There's a hospital in Junction City. Number 7 will take you there in a couple of hours."

"They'll kick me out." The man grinned wryly. "No money. Can't even pay my fare."

Ace kicked the door closer and lifted the man's legs up on it. "You'll learn to draw pay in advance when you're hired to kill a man," he said.

"I did. But that was yesterday. I played poker in Jake's place last night."

"Serves you right! Well, when you get well you can come back and tell me about it, if you want to." Ace turned and walked down the platform toward the incoming train. A door midway down the line of cars was open and as the train stopped a man in blue coat with brass buttons stepped down and dropped a box-step.

"Howdy, Jim. I got a passenger for you. Help me load him on, will you?"

"Hello, Ace!" The conductor glanced past Gilbert to the wounded man. "What's goin' on? Gettin' so yuh can't bury yuhr own dead, or somethin'?"

"He's alive." A pair of trim silk stockings came down the steps into the range of Gilbert's vision, but he did not look up. "Want you to take him to the Junction. Wire ahead to have 'em send an ambulance from the hospital to meet him. Tell 'em I'll pay the bills. How much will the fare be?"

"Dollar ninety. There's a doctor on the train, Ace. Feller from Usted. Maybe he could fix this hombre up?"

"Have him try. Pay him and send me the bill . . . Here, you take his feet." They stooped together and lifted the door as a stretcher. The silk stockings had come all the way down the steps now and two small grey shoes halted beside Ace as he straightened with his load. Another passenger was leaving the train now, too; a man.

"You can't go on ignoring me, you know, Lord Gil!" There was a musical something in the low, even voice that was familiar. Ace Gilbert recognized it even before he saw her face; before the tell-tale "Lord Gil" that could come from no one else. "You took one look at my legs as I came down the steps and turned right away without even risking a further glance! Were they so bad that you didn't consider it worth while, or what?"

"Hello, Kay!" He paused in mid-stride forgetting his burden. The conductor rammed his middle against the end of the door and said something that sounded mildly profane. Ace grinned, suddenly. "Not bad at all," he said. "So good I was afraid to look up for fear the face wouldn't match 'em. . . . Be back in a minute, infant."

He was still grinning when he passed the man who had been Kay Cameron's fellow passenger. The man was a stranger; tall, broad-shouldered, with a thin, well-bred looking face. Ace had an impression of loosely fitting clothes and a wisp of blond mustache trimmed close over a well-shaped mouth. The man was looking curiously at the wounded man on the litter so that his glance did not meet Gilbert's at all.

They laid the wounded man on the long, leather couch in the smoking compartment of one of the cars and the conductor departed at once in search of the doctor. Ace thrust a folded bill in the wounded one's hand. "They'll take care of you," he said. "If you feel like it, later, you might come back and have a talk with me. Or write. Ace Gilbert, care of the Lazy 9, will get me. So long, and— good luck!"

The train was moving now and Ace stepped back into the corridor and ran for the door. The man on the couch in the compartment he had just left lifted the folded bill above his face and stared at it. "Well, I'll be damned!" he said softly.

Ace swung down from the moving train at the eastern end of the platform and turned back to meet the owner of the silken legs. She put out both her hands to him and he took them eagerly, holding her at arm's length. "Why, Kay, you've grown up! Lord, you look fine! Where'd you drop from, anyway? Thought you were learning your a, b, c's or something, on the coast!"

"You called me infant a while ago," she said accusingly. "Take it back?"

"I'll have to, sure! It's great to see you, Kay!"

"Are you really glad, Ace?"

He nodded.

"Glad as you look?"

He nodded again.

"It'll be all right to kiss me then!" she said, judiciously. "After all, you're practically one of the family!"

He pulled her toward him and hugged her tight, laughing; tilted her face up and planted a kiss squarely on her lips. There was something about that kiss that startled him a little, and he kissed her again by way of research. Her lips were softer than Ruth's somehow; seemed to cling, sort of. . . .

"Heavens! As a brotherly caress that was—well, *thorough*, at any rate!" She looked up at him, pursing her lips a little, thoughtfully. "Do you kiss Ruth like that, Ace? Or dare I ask?"

"Not many things you don't dare, imp! Sure I kiss Ruth like that! Why?"

"Then I wonder why she went to Europe." She put one finger against her cheek and frowned. Ace Gilbert's look was too much for her and she broke away from him, laughing. "Never mind, Lord Gil! It was nice of you to meet me, anyway. Don't tell me you didn't do it intentionally! Don't say you came down here merely to shoot somebody and that meeting me was an accident!"

"I beg your pardon?" The tall man with the mustache interposed before Ace could answer and they turned toward him inquiringly. "You see, I thought Buffalo Wells was a town of some sort, and not . . ." He lifted his shoulders and hands in an expressive gesture that took in the emptiness about them. "I supposed there'd be people, and a hotel, and some sort of conveyance to take me where I want to go. So I didn't wire ahead that I was coming, and naturally no one is meeting me. Will I starve, do you think, before I'm rescued?" He smiled, and there was something in the smile that won their liking.

Ace chuckled. "I reckon it won't be as bad as that," he said. "That cloud of dust yonder is the stage from the Wells. It'll be here soon; can't imagine why it's late, anyway. . . . My name is Asher Gilbert. If you'd tell me who your friends are I might be able to get word to them."

"Thank you. I'm Gordon Wallace, Mr. Gilbert. I'm visiting the Camerons; Senator Cameron's family, you know. I think their ranch is called the Triangle, or . . ."

"Triangle is right!" Ace turned to Kay, puzzled a little "This is Miss Kathryn Cameron, Mr. Wallace. You—haven't met?"

"Well, that's a coincidence, isn't it? No, I haven't had the pleasure. It is a pleasure, too, Miss Kathryn! . . . You see, it was Miss Ruth Cameron who was kind enough to invite me here. Your sister, perhaps?"

"Yes." Kay shot a sidelong glance at Ace before extending her hand. "You knew Ruth at college, perhaps?"

"Unfortunately, no. I went to Oxford, and I don't imagine that Miss Ruth did, since she told me that this was her first time abroad. We crossed from Peking together, as a matter of fact. I met your sister there. My business in San Francisco couldn't be settled at once, and when I learned that, I hopped a train and came on."

The buckboard that served as a stage between the station and town drew up to the end of the platform with a flourish and two men climbed down. One of them was the station agent, and a third horse on a lead-rope behind the stage offered a clue to his previous absence. Ace lifted Kay Cameron's bags and walked down toward them. The agent bustled about the lead horse, jerking at the bridle to force the beast up to the rack. "First time I've missed a train in a year and more," he said volubly. "Damn plug! Think yuh're a blasted outlaw, or something, eh? At yuhr age!"

"What's wrong, Jenkins?" Ace lifted the bags to the back of the buckboard as he addressed the irate agent.

"Ah, I spent the night in town and started t' ride back this mornin' and this fool horse piled me! Wouldn't even let me catch him, afterward! Acted like a fool colt! I'd be chasin' him yet, likely, if Hank hadn't come by with the stage and helped me out!"

Ace squinted sideways at the horse; an ancient, sad-eyed beast with no hint of any such youthful deviltry in his looks, certainly. "Never bucked before, did he?" His question was quite casual.

"No! Man my age's got no use fer a buckin' horse, has he? 'F he'd done it before I'd-a sold him! Gonna sell him now, 'f anyone'll make me an offer!"

Ace walked past the little man and laid a hand on the horse's rump. The beast humped himself and stepped aside. Ace stooped and loosened the cinches, speaking to the horse as he worked. He lifted the saddle then and laid it across the hitching bar. There was a clean knife-cut in the thick felt on the under side of the saddle and Ace pulled the padding aside. "Thought so," he said.

"Somebody cut the felt and slid a burr under it. Took it a while to work through, but when it did the horse pitched. Can't blame him." He tossed the burr away and let the padding drop into place again. "He won't pitch any more," he said.

"What'd anybody do a thing like that for, anyway?" The agent stared at Gilbert in gaping amazement. "Yuh reckon they thought that was a *joke?* Dammit, s'pose there'd been a stop order fer Number 7 and me not here t' take it! Maybe there was! Maybe she's runnin' slam into a head-on with somethin' now! Helluva joke, that'd be, wouldn't it?"

"It wasn't a joke, exactly." Ace's right hand went up unconsciously to the rent in his shirt where the stranger's lead had cut. "Somebody wanted to make sure you wouldn't be here this mornin', that's all. You haven't a registered package here for me, have you?"

The agent shook his head dumbly.

"Thought not! The same somebody that put the burr in your saddle left word there was a package here that I'd have to sign for. There was a man lyin' for me when I got here." He glanced at Kay and wondered a bit at the sudden pallor of her cheeks. "It was him I just put on the train," he said. "Climb up, Mr. Wallace. This man will take you to the Wells. Here, Kay; up you go! I'll ride beside you."

He mounted Satan and rolled a cigarette while the stage driver received the mail sacks and turned his team back toward the town. The white horse swung in abreast of the passengers' seat and Ace swung one leg over his saddle horn. "How-come nobody's down to meet you, Kay?" he asked. "There was a mob here yesterday when Ruth came in."

"Much enthusiasm on the part of the Cameron retainers, I suppose? Fine bunch they must be, too, now that Wes Luckert has fired all the old boys! Why should I bid for a welcome from men I never saw?" She tossed her head impatiently, "I didn't tell anyone I was coming, Ace. . . . Who is it that's gunning for you, and why?"

Gilbert's lips tightened a little. "Never saw him before. Texas man, judgin' from his talk."

"Don't sidestep! That doesn't answer either of my questions, and you know it! What happened on Thunder River, anyway?"

Ace shrugged. "Some rustlin' goin' on. Rumors flyin' around. Nothin' much."

Kay Cameron nodded. "Two or three fair-sized rumors landed on you, if one may judge by your looks, no? One grazed your lip and one left a beautiful bruise on your jaw!"

Ace grinned sheepishly but said nothing. Gordon Wallace leaned forward and spoke past Kay. "Mind clearing me up a bit, Gilbert? Do I understand you've just escaped a deliberate attempt on your life, or something? This business of the burr in our friend's saddle, and the chap you carried on the train—something about a trap, wasn't it?"

Ace grinned. "Looks that way, all right. Somebody left word for me to come down to sign for a registered package, and when I got here the station was empty. I heard a horse move back of the shack, and felt this hombre watchin' me."

"And what did you do? Go on! Confound it, man, don't stop there, will you?"

"Turned around and took a shot at him. Jumped over the track and ducked. Tossed a rock through a window and stood up while he was lookin' at the broken glass. He missed, and I didn't. That's all."

Gordon Wallace threw his head back and laughed delightedly. "Splendid!" he said. "Very simple and efficient! Nothing to it at all! Oh, no! By George, Gilbert, I'm going to like you, rather!"

There was honest admiration in the man's tone and Ace flushed a little, finding no answer ready. Kay Cameron glanced sidelong at her seat companion with new approval in her eyes. This man might be the cause of an embarrassing situation in the Cameron family, but at least he was wholesome and man-sized. "The elder Cameron girl has taste," she told herself, silently, "even if she does lack discretion! . . . Ace Gilbert and Gordon Wallace! Well, it's a pair to draw to, anyway!"

And so it was a foursome rather than a duet that rode out of the Wells just after noon that day on the way to the Triangle; Kay Cameron and Gordon Wallace on mounts hired from the livery and Ruth and Ace on the sorrel and Satan.

Wallace looked well in riding gear, Ace thought; nothing comic about clothes like that on a man who fitted them. The stranger used shorter stirrups than were approved in the West, and he rose to the trot in a way that embarrassed his mount somewhat; but he had a good seat and steady hands.

Just how it occurred Ace did not know, but the foursome had divided from the start into twos, with Ruth paired with Gordon in the lead and her sister bringing up the rear with Ace. The latter rode in silence for a time, Kay Cameron watching Gilbert's face from the corner of her eyes.

"Nice couple," she said at last.

Ace started slightly. "Yes," he admitted tersely.

"Ruth has a way of carrying off embarrassing moments, hasn't she? I'd have been flustered as the devil with a steamship beau dropping in on me when I'd been away from the husband-to-be for a year."

"I can't picture you gettin' flustered," Ace answered.

Kay did a make-shift curtsy, if a curtsy on horseback is possible. "Thank you, kind sir," she said. "I know now which rumor it was that landed on your jaw," she added irrelevantly. "It was evidently something of a blow to the rumor, too!"

Ace met her gaze inquiringly now. "Saw Wes, did you? . . . Ruth didn't like my minglin' in a public brawl, I reckon. I'm bein' punished." He glanced at the pair ahead and grinned a little ruefully. "I'm sorry, but Wes asked for what he got, Kay."

"Are you telling me, Lord Gil? He's been asking for it for years! . . . But I still don't see why he wants you killed, Ace. That's carrying it a bit far, isn't it?"

Ace frowned at her. "What put that in your head?" he asked.

"I've been to school, you know! Two and two make four in any language!"

"First, you need one and one to make two, though. For a little girl you do have the funniest notions, imp! Why in the world would Wes want to kill me?"

"I can think of several reasons! If you don't stop treating me like a five-year-old I'm apt to side with Wes myself! Can't you forget, please, that you used to jiggle me on your knee and buy me lollypops?"

"Nope." Ace Gilbert's blue eyes twinkled mirthfully at the angry gleam in Kay's dark ones. "My heart turns flip-flops at the mere thought of jigglin' you on my knee, Kay! That's an old habit we ought to practice up on, eh, imp?"

"If we do, Asher Gilbert, you'll find out that I *am* grown up! . . . In more ways than one!" she added darkly.

"I'm not doubtin' it," he told her seriously, remembering her kiss a while ago.

"Now, what do you mean by that?" she asked, her eyes on him still but with a different light in them than had been there up to now. But Ace answered her with a shrug and she did not press the question. Perhaps she guessed his meaning, and preferred it left unsaid.

The ride ended at last at the Triangle, and Ace Gilbert retained his seat on the stallion while the rest swung down. "Thanks, Ruth, but I can't stay," he said in answer to Ruth Cameron's invitation for the afternoon. "Been away since yesterday mornin' you know, and the boys'll be ridin' in after me if I don't show up. I'll be over soon, though; tomorrow, maybe; or next day."

She nodded and turned away. "It's good to be home," she said. "Come soon, Asher, won't you? We'll need you to help us show Gordon about."

Ace nodded and swung the stallion about. He halted again as Wallace called him, waiting as the man walked back toward him. Gordon Wallace's face was very solemn now and he did not speak until he stood at Gilbert's stirrup.

"I'm afraid I'm a butter-in, old chap," he said, slowly. "You see, I didn't know when I came that there was a fiancé in the offing; that sort of thing. Ruth was telling me, just now." He paused, a bit uncertain as to choice of words. "What's the best thing, d'you think? Do I make my bow and gallop off stage, or—not? You see, Gilbert, it happens that I—I love her, too!"

He said it simply; earnestly; meeting Gilbert's eyes with steady candor as he spoke. "Seemed the only sporting thing, telling you. Say the word and I'll clear out, of course. Utmost respect for you, and all that sort of thing. But a man would like the chance to play out his turn, naturally. Up to you."

There was silence between them for a moment. Ace Gilbert put out his hand. "You're a white man, Wallace," he said. "Play your hand, of course! It's a fair field and no favor, I reckon. And—may the best man win!"

Wallace struck his hand into Gilbert's outstretched one and gripped it hard. "Sportsman!" he said tersely. "And about that best-man-winning thing. . . . Sorry. Can't subscribe to that, I'm afraid! Want to win myself, if I can! . . . Thanks, Gilbert. I was right in thinking I'd like you!"

There was a tiny, puzzled frown on Ace Gilbert's face as the white horse lifted him away and bore him down toward the Lazy 9; and there was the memory, too, in his fingers of a hard, strong hand that had met his own in a frank, firm clasp. "Sportsman," he repeated softly. "It's a good word, sure! . . . I reckon the likin' is goin' to be mutual, amigo—*either way!*"

# 5 • "FERGUSON'S NEGRO"

SATAN'S PROGRESS southward might have seemed slow and needlessly round-about to anyone who had heard Ace Gilbert's excuse for immediate departure from the Triangle. For one whose presence on the Lazy 9 was urgent and imperative, Ace chose a devious course that ignored the direct, well-worn trail and sought instead the winding highlands from which he might overlook the range. Wes Luckert had left the Wells last night, he knew; and there had been no visible evidence of his presence at the Triangle today. Which meant simply that Luckert was on the range somewhere. No better or more proper place for a range boss than his own range, certainly; but after the incident at the station this morning it seemed to Ace Gilbert that due caution was the better part of valor. The direct route between the Triangle and the Lazy 9 might be as safe today as it had been those countless other times in the past when he had ridden it, or it might hold a rendezvous with death.

Strange that Ruth Cameron hadn't told Wallace that she was engaged. They had met on the boat; or possibly in Peking, before sailing. Time enough, surely, for her to mention a fiancé if they had been at all intimate. Perhaps that was it; perhaps they had been casual, shipboard acquaintances between whom confidences might not be exchanged? Ace frowned a little, doubtfully. Those shipboard things were sudden and intense, according to the books; and this one had been serious enough to warrant an invitation to the Triangle, at least. Wallace loved the girl, he said; and he was hardly the man to conceal his feelings in a matter like that when time was limited to the space of an ocean crossing. Ruth must have known, Ace thought. Why hadn't she told Wallace that the game was already lost?

Of course the thing might have seemed no more than the usual ship flirtation to her. Even her invitation to the Triangle might have been one of those small courtesies of parting which are offered casually and forgotten. The delay in Wallace's business and his decision to accept the invitation might have been a complete surprise to Ruth; and she had told him the truth immediately on his arrival, at least. Of course, she could hardly have avoided it then, with Gilbert quite evidently on the ground! She must know how he felt now, certainly; and she had not sent him away. It seemed hardly fair, to be entirely frank about it; not quite—sporting, to use Wallace's own term.

The criticism was no sooner formed in his mind than Ace cast it aside and reviled himself mentally for having entertained it at all. If Ruth knew how Wallace felt toward her, as she must now, it would have been nothing less than crude—even cruel—to send him packing at once. The high regard of a man like Wallace was an honor, certainly; deserved a girl's respect. Ruth would appreciate that, and would wish to soften the hurt. It was the decent, proper thing to do. No sense in blaming her for it, like a jealous child begrudging the use of a toy.

And so Ace forced the doubt from his mind and called himself a fool. It was great to have her home, anyway. No more lonely weeks for him now; with Ruth within riding distance. Ruth, and Kay. It was the first time in two years that Kay had been on the Triangle. Last summer, he remembered, she had spent the holidays with some friend on the coast. How she had grown! What was it she had said in answer to his joking offer to renew an old practice of jiggling on his knee? "If we do, Asher Gilbert, you'll find out that I *am* grown up! . . . In more ways than one!"

"I wonder what she meant by that?" he mused. "She'd be a hundred and ten pounds now, instead of sixty-odd; that's one way. . . . Shucks! No tellin' what that kid means! She's sure turned into a pretty one, though. No spindle-shanked tomboy about her now!" The thought reminded him of his first glimpse of her and he chuckled over the question she had asked about her legs. "Nothin' wrong with them, I'll tell a man! And she knows it, too."

Ace brought his thoughts back to the rustling problem again. Dave Robertson had mentioned Buck Wilbur and his gang. But Ace couldn't take that very seriously. Buck Wilbur was a noted desperado, cattle thief and bank robber, a cold-blooded killer. With his henchman Farley, who was said to do most of his dirty work for him, Wilbur had terrorized Arizona a few years back. Nothing had been heard of him since then. There had even been a rumor that Wilbur had died, obscurely and ingloriously, in a brawl in some gaming house of a small mining town. Farley seemed to have dropped from view completely. Ace thought Robertson was seeing things, suspecting Wilbur as the cause of the recent depredations of stock. Wilbur would never dare to show himself around these parts. His face had been blazened on too many posters in the sheriffs' offices of four states. Unless he were holed up in the hills, and letting others do his work for him in town, Wilbur could not be the man at the bottom of the trouble. For it seemed to Ace that the man or men who were behind the present ruckus were stirring up more than the stealing of a few head of cattle had so far indicated. Well, he'd wait and watch, and see what he could see.

The ridge on which he rode ended abruptly in a steep promontory that slanted down to a dry creek bed where, in rainy times, a tributary cut its way to Thunder River further south. There were sparse trees along the cutbanks, and just under the nose of the ridge a tight thicket of underbrush blocked the way down to the wash. Satan swung east a little, paralleling the tangle to a point where a cattle trail led through to a deeper hole in the gulch where water might sometimes be found even after the stream was dead. There was water there now, and the trail through the thicket showed the marks of cattle's hoofs.

A burly calf whirled from the stagnant water to face

the intruder as Satan cleared the brushy screen about the
hole, and Ace read with the instinct of the cattleman
the marks on the youngster's ear. Sharped right, swallow-
fork left; the Triangle mark. The calf was a shorthorn—
one of the crop of half-bred stock from the expensive
bulls with which Cameron had stocked his range; an
ugly youngster, this one, with a spooky cast about the
eyes. Ace remembered him instantly as one he had
hazed back across the river after finding him on the
Lazy 9 range a month or so ago. The calf whirled awkwardly and plunged down the side of the wash. Ace
stared after him for a moment, his eyes suddenly narrowed and thoughtful.

"That's funny," he said softly. "Come on, white horse;
let's give that critter a run!"

The stallion made short work of the gulch and
stretched nimbly on the other side in pursuit of the calf.
They headed the fugitive from the left, and as he
turned, Ace swung the horse sharply to gain a view of
the calf's off side. He reined up then, watching the calf
make off among the trees.

"Funnier than I thought," he said, finally. "That critter was branded, all right, last time I saw him."

There was no doubt about the round-about course to
which Satan was put between that water hole and the
river, but now there was no loitering on the way. Ace
rode a mile directly out of his course to gain a ridge
this time, and half a dozen times after that he rode an
equal distance to one side or the other to pass near a
group of grazing stock. Once, having trapped a frightened calf against its fellows, he rode alongside and
stooped low from the saddle to run his hand along the
youngster's side. When he straightened after that his face
was very stern, and he drew rein sharply to roll a cigaret
while the frightened cattle slowed further on and stopped
to stare back at him wonderingly.

It was dark when he reached the Lazy 9 that evening
and the men were already grouped around the wash-
stand outside the bunkhouse when he rode past them
toward the barn. He answered their greetings shortly

and dismounted at the stable, leading Satan in to the box stall that was kept apart for him. He groomed the horse carefully and measured out a feed of oats into the box; opened the stall door to the corral where Satan would find water and hay. The men were already at table when he had done, and he slid into his place at the head of the board.

"Satan go lame on yuh, Ace?" Timothy O'Keefe, Gilbert's foreman, looked up inquiringly, speaking through a mouthful of beans.

"Didn't your ma ever tell you not to talk with your mouth full?" Ace wanted to know reprovingly. "No, Satan didn't go lame. Why?"

"Sure took yuh a long time t' ride out from town," O'Keefe suggested, slyly. "Thought maybe Satan was limpin', or somethin'."

"Go to hell, Tim," Ace advised mildly. "I rode out to the Triangle with Ruth. Kay's home, too, by the way. Plumb grown up, Kay is. Pretty as can be."

"Who was tellin' yuh about Kay, anyway?" O'Keefe spoke with the privilege of friendship that had nothing to do with the status of employer and employee. "Yuh was so busy oglin' Miss Ruth I'm surprised yuh even seen Kay!" He washed the beans down with a draught of coffee and spoke more intelligibly for it. "Jimmy White rode by 'safternoon," he said, squinting at Ace thoughtfully. "From town," he added. "How'd yuh get all bruised that way, Ace? Run into a door in the dark?"

"If Jimmy White was here," Ace told him, "you'd know what door I hit!" He frowned and changed the subject quickly. "By the way, Tim. Remember that cock-eyed doggie we hazed over the river four-five weeks ago? One of Cameron's shorthorns?"

"Yeah." O'Keefe was disinterested.

"Remember if he was branded or not?"

O'Keefe glanced up and looked back again at his plate. "Must'a been, since we knowed he was Triangle," he said. "Yeah, he was branded; ear-marked, too."

"I saw him today. He's still ear-marked, but he must've rubbed his brand off on a tree, maybe!"

A full dozen pairs of eyes searched Gilbert's face from about the table now, and the noise of eating was stilled. "Maybe he swapped hides with another calf," O'Keefe suggested.

"Or maybe he was wearin' a hair brand when we saw him. I found a calf running with Triangle stuff just after I saw this one—a calf with a mighty tough hide, this was. The brandin' iron hadn't even raised a welt on him!"

Timothy O'Keefe took another mouthful of beans and assimilated them slowly. "I always said Luckert was a skunk," he said, when they were gone.

A youngster further down the table spoke up curiously.

"Why would they hair-brand 'em, Ace? Why not put their iron on 'em the first time? Hair brandin' means double handlin' and double risk!"

O'Keefe favored the speaker with a scathing frown. "*And* double profits," he said. "The biggest drawback t' rustlin', young feller, is the fact that calves run with their ma till they're weaned, and mostly they're branded before that time. Branded with the same iron that's on the old cow, sabe? Them as gets overlooked is mavericks, and the percentage o' mavericks on a range like this is small."

"Go on, teacher. Damn it, Tim, I know all that. . . ."

"Shut up and listen t' yuhr betters, Eddy, me lad! As I was sayin', the percentage o' mavericks on a good range is small, and they ain't enough of 'em to keep a real industrious rustler busy. So, if he's real smart and has the chance, Mr. Rustler is apt t' hair-brand a few calves; lay the iron on 'em light, so the brand ain't burned in, sabe? Then, any honest puncher seein' the calf sees him branded with the same brand that's on the cow he's runnin' with, and that's one less to rope. Mr. Calf gets weaned and purty soon he sheds his coat—and presto-chango he's a maverick! Course he's ear-marked, makin' him a sleeper; but the rustlin' hombre can come along now and work over his ears and slap a brand on him, and Mr. Rustler has him a beef! Simple, ain't it? Next lesson'll be how t' eat beans with a knife, 'thout cuttin' yuhr throat!"

reproachfully, ~~...~~ boys are goin' to be real busy ~~...~~ ~~...~~kin' for that star-faced bull I bought from Ca~~...~~ ~~...~~st fall. Like as not he'd head back to his home range. While you're huntin' him you can take a squint at any Triangle calves you run across, too. Be interestin' to know if this hair-brandin' is gettin' common on the Triangle range. It'd be just as well if you wasn't seen, maybe; but if anybody asks you, you're lookin' for that bull. Sabe?"

"That star-faced devil is on the south range, Ace." The lad called Ed put his head in the noose again and O'Keefe whooped derisively. Ace nodded.

"I know he is, Ed," he said. "But you'll be lookin' for him up north, see? Won't be your fault if a fool bull don't know where you're lookin', will it?"

The meal was concluded shortly and the Lazy 9 riders filed out, leaving Ace Gilbert and Tim O'Keefe at the table alone. O'Keefe rubbed his jaw reflectively and frowned. "Hair-brandin' can't get by, o' course, unless a range boss is blind in both eyes or don't want t' see," he said. "Wes Luckert ain't blind. Which means he's in it himself; that he's swellin' his own private Horseshoe brand by stealin' Triangle calves; which proves that he's a skunk like I said a while ago. Steve Cameron picked Wes up when he was nothin' but a range bum and made a range boss out o' him. Gratitude, eh? Humph! . . . But just the same, Ace, yuh ain't lettin' the Luckert scent, rank as it is, toll yuh off the main trail, are yuh? As the feller said there's b'ar in them mountains, even if Luckert *is* messin' up the track with skunk-scent!"

"Meanin'?"

"Meanin' Buck Wilbur and his wild bunch. There's bear for yuh; *honest* cow-thieves that ain't botherin' with hair-brandin' and all them fancy twists!"

"Dave Robertson mentioned that, yesterday. . . . How do we know Buck Wilbur's in the hills, Tim? Give a dog a bad name, you know, and he gets the blame no matter t to mention such ... and train hold-ups. He got to be ... figure when Farley brought the gang into a little Arizona town, and terrorized it, to yank Wilbur out of jail the night before he was to hang; and since then he's been blamed for every two-bit crime that's been done between here and the Pecos! Every time a cow critter falls in a bog and disappears there's a yell goes up about Buck Wilbur and Farley and his wild bunch! . . . Sure, there's men in the hills here that are stealin' cattle; but that don't prove that Buck Wilbur's doin' it, does it?"

"That don't, no. Yuh happen t' remember, Ace, how they caught Wilbur that time, before the jail-breaks?"

"Why, yes. They got one of his gang first, didn't they? A black man, I think it was. He turned state's evidence; told them where to locate his boss."

"Right. There was a Negro killed up north couple o' weeks ago, Ace. He was workin' for a man named Ferguson; old time cattleman, Ferguson is, but he got smashed up when a horse fell with him and he's runnin' some sheep in a big valley up there. This Negro was helpin' him. They got a couple o' collie dogs handlin' them sheep that's got more brains than most humans. Well, Ferguson's got a daughter named Mary, and I was up t' see her last night" . . . O'Keefe avoided Gilbert's eye, frowning to hide a too-evident embarrassment; "and she was tellin' me about this Negro bein' killed. Seems like he didn't show up one night when the dogs brought the woolies home, and the next day Ferguson goes out with the dogs and finds him. He'd been beat up terrible, and shot to pieces besides. He was still breathin' when Ferguson found him, but he died right soon after. 'Fore he passed out he recognized Ferguson and said a few words. Said it was Buck Wilbur's gang that got him; said Buck swore he'd do it after the Negro squealed on him, and the Negro had left Arizona on that account. Seems Wilbur or one of his men located the Negro somehow, and made good his threat."

"Why hasn't this man, Ferguson, reported that to the sheriff? He hasn't or I'd have heard about it in town."

"No, he ain't reported it. Can't blame him, either, Ace. He's alone up there, him and his girl; and he's just had a sample o' what Wilbur does to folks that talk too much. I want their names kept out of it, myself, Ace. They was trustin' me to protect 'em when they told me, and I aim to do it."

Gilbert nodded. "She must be a right pretty girl, Tim," he said.

O'Keefe flushed and stood up. "She is," he admitted.

"What the devil was the idea, though, of lettin' me shoot off my mouth the way I did to prove that Wilbur *wasn't* in the hills when you knew all the time that he *was?*" Ace bent a suspicious gaze on his foreman now, and O'Keefe sidled toward the door.

"Yuh plumb spellbound me with yuhr oratory, Ace," he said. "If yuh talk like that t' Miss Ruth I can't sabe how she's resisted yuh as long as she has! It must be a gift. . . ."

A loaf of bread from the table grazed O'Keefe's shoulder as he plunged for the door and Gilbert's outraged voice pursued him. "Get out o' here, before I make you a gift of a poke in the nose! . . . Thanks, Tim, for tellin' me!"

# 6 · STEVE CAMERON

ACE GILBERT found no time during the day that followed for a visit to the Triangle. The knowledge of the presence on Thunder River of Buck Wilbur, Arizona's champion rustler and most audacious outlaw, changed

Ace's outlook on the whole situation, and changed it materially. With Buck Wilbur loose in the Mescaleros there were no grounds for minimizing the reports of cattle losses on the ranges lying closest to the hills. Any losses at all could mean only one thing: that Wilbur had gathered, or was gathering, an outlaw band with which to scourge the cattle lands along Thunder River as he had scourged the southwestern ranges five years ago.

And yet, Ace was puzzled. It scarcely seemed possible that Wilbur would be able to operate here without being seen and recognized by someone. The Negro who had been shot down had named Wilbur's gang as his assassins; he had not specified Wilbur himself. And Wilbur was unmistakable. Outlaw and bandit, he had nevertheless been a picturesque figure, with flaming hair that seemed to exaggerate the largeness of his head, all out of proportion to the slight wiriness of his body. Ace had seen innumerable pictures of him. His gang had remained more shadowy, a colorless background of grim men, tagged with names that struck fear—One-shot Farley, said to have the quickest draw in seven states; Dynamite Burton, clever at blowing the toughest safes wide open—and many others, whose names were known, but whose faces had faded from sight behind the brilliance and the striking color of their leader. And yet, if somehow, Wilbur were here? Unless he were stopped before he regained his oldtime strength and audacity, no brand within a hundred miles of his stronghold would be safe from his raids. Instead of minor depredations limited to the ranges closest to the hills would come sweeping round-ups by hard-riding crews that would close like a drag-net about a hundred head of cattle at a time; a drag-net that would pay no heed to human obstacles other than the scant attention needed to kill. Buck Wilbur's trail in Arizona had been thickly strewn with murdered men who had interfered. Riders on night herds had been shot down unwarned as Wilbur's raiders swooped down upon their herds. Trainmen and mailclerks had been killed coldbloodedly in the course of train robberies. Bank cashiers and guards had gone down before the fire of Wilbur's men as they gutted vaults and safes. There had been no quarter in Wilbur's methods then, and there would be none now. A wolf seldom changes his methods of hunting.

And so Ace Gilbert rode his range carefully throughout that day and the next, locating his herds and gauging their liability to attack while at the same time he searched for signs that might indicate a raid already made. He had told Robertson, in town, that the Lazy 9 had suffered no losses. He had believed and still hoped that that was true; but on a range as large as his a minor loss might go unnoticed for a time at least and he wished now to verify his hope.

It occurred to him now that the news of Buck Wilbur's presence in the hills had driven from his mind for the moment his suspicions regarding Wes Luckert. More than suspicions, they were, really. Two or three of the Lazy 9 men had ridden in last night to report and Ace had met two others today as he skirted the river. The two "sleepers" he had seen himself were only two of many his men had seen since. Certainly there were more of them than any range could harbor without the knowledge of the man in charge.

Luckert's thievery, if it were proved to be that, would, however, be only a minor thing beside the greater threat from the hills. Ruth Cameron had said on her arrival that her father would return to the Triangle within a day or so, and when he came Ace would pass his discovery along. He disliked the rôle of the informer, but certainly his allegiance belonged first to the Camerons without regard to his status with Luckert. Soon now he would himself be responsible for the Triangle as well as for the Lazy 9, for it was Steve Cameron's expressed desire that the two brands should be handled as one after Ruth and Ace Gilbert were married; so that Gilbert's interest could hardly be termed interference.

It was late afternoon of the second day since his return from town when Ace turned Satan northward across the river toward the triangle. He had found nothing to indicate that any of his herds were depleted, and he had laid out in his mind a campaign of defense that might serve to protect them later. By combining the cattle into two or three large and centrally located herds under constant guard he could at least make the rustler's task a difficult one. The guards would have strict orders not to fight, he decided. He would not risk the lives of his men in any such one-sided battle, to have them shot down as men had been shot down in the southwest by these same night-riding killers. The guard would be set for the purpose of reporting the raid. If Wilbur's outfit struck one herd, its guards would ride to notify the men guarding the other two. Then, with his forces gathered, Ace would intercept the raiders if he could and force a battle of his own choosing.

The Triangle ranch yard was seemingly deserted as Ace rode into it and it was not until he had dismounted before the house that he saw the still figure seated, chin in hands and elbows on knees, upon the porch. It was Kay, and she eyed him disapprovingly as he came up the path toward her.

"Picture the ardent lover come a-wooing!" she said. "For pete's sake, Lord Gil, is this your idea of a tempestuous courtship? Is this your idea of sweeping a girl off her feet?"

He sat down beside her, laughing a little. "Why, what's wrong, imp? You mad at me about somethin'? . . . Where's Ruth?"

"Ruth's out somewhere with Gordon, and serves you damn well right, sez I! You might at least have come staggering in with a broken leg, or an arm, as an excuse for your absence! Or were you restraining your ardor for the sake of formality—with a girl to whom you've been engaged for fourteen months?"

"Shucks, Kay, I intended to get up here sooner, but things at the ranch had to be 'tended to and I couldn't get away. Ruth won't mind. I reckon she's been busy anyway, entertainin' Wallace."

" 'Ruth won't mind,' eh?" she mimicked him. "Well, maybe you know; but if *I* were engaged to a man, and

I'd been away 'most a year, and when I came home he waited two whole days before he paid his call . . ."

"I'd have come if I could, Kay. Business before pleasure, you know. . . ."

"Piffle! What's business compared to love? Ask any girl! Oh, business is all right, of course; but a girl wants to be the most important thing in a man's life, Ace, for a while at least! If a man loved me, I'd want him to flatter me by being an utter fool about me sometimes! I'd want him to bully me, and humor me, and let business go hang to be with me, and . . ." Words failed her and she made an eloquent little gesture with her hands. "You see? 'Lessons in Love, by Kay Cameron!' No extra charge!"

"Yes, you *would* want—that," he said slowly. Perhaps she imagined it, but Kay thought there was a wistful something in his voice just then; a something that gave meaning to his next sure statement. "But Ruth doesn't." He faced her now, his face entirely sober and intent. "You're mighty different, you two—for sisters. I wonder —would you want a man to—kiss you, Kay, if you hadn't seen him for a long time—even if there were people watching, and . . . you know what I mean." His eyes dropped before her steady gaze and he felt hot blood at his cheeks.

Kay did not answer for a moment. "So *that's* it!" she told herself, silently. "He kissed her, and it upset her dignity! Oh, Ruth, you little fool! You—fool!" And then, at last, to Ace: "Of course I would, Ace. I'd be glad he cared enough not to mind who saw . . ." She stumbled a little; caught herself gallantly. "Ruth is very proud, Ace; reserved, and—dignified. Almost prim, sometimes. But she's awf'ly fine. It's just that I'm—the brat of the family, you know! Nobody'd expect me to be like Ruth!"

He smiled at her gently. "Nobody'd want you to be like anybody but you," he said. "You're pretty sweet as you are, you know . . . I reckon they'll be back before very long, won't they? Ruth and Wallace, I mean?"

She turned her face away from him, fearful of what there might be in her eyes. "You mustn't say sweet noth-

ings like that to me, Lord Gil," she said. In her heart,
she phrased it differently, but he should not know that
it was his instant return to thoughts of Ruth that had
hurt her. "Yes, they'll be back soon. You'd better wait.
Now that you're here it wouldn't do to go chasing off
again without seeing her!"

"Sure, I'll wait . . . Wallace is a pretty good sort, isn't
he? I liked him, just at first glance."

"You'll like him at second glance, too. He's all right.
Maybe some good brisk competition will pep you up a
little as a lover, Lord Gil! He's that, you know!" She
grinned at him impudently, and they laughed together
as they had done since the days when she was a child.

"Yes, I know," he said. "He told me! I liked that,
too. . . . When will the Colonel be back, Kay? Ruth
said you expected him in a day or so."

"Dad? Oh, tonight or tomorrow, I think. He'll be
surprised to find me here!" She chuckled boyishly.
"He raved because I wouldn't come home, but he finally
wired me money to spend the summer with some girls
in 'Frisco; and now when he comes he'll find me here
after all! I'm going to keep the money, though! Spotty's
getting old and he deserves a rest anyway; so I'm having Tony break a new mount for me, and I'm going to
have a new saddle and boots and a Stetson with my
vacation money. Handmade boots, I'll have you know;
and ditto saddle—with a martingale, and white buckskin
trim!"

"Regular dude, aren't you, imp? You ought to have a
white horse to go with a rig like that, though. Say! I've
got a red and white pinto three-year-old that'd be just
your size, Kay! One of Satan's sons, out of that little sorrel I used to ride in the sprint races; remember? I'll
bring him up next time I come and if you like him you
can tell Tony not to bother breakin' one for you. How's
that?"

"Grand, Ace! I've always wanted one of Satan's colts.
Gee, Ace, I'll love it!" She paused for a moment, her
eyes dancing impishly. "You—sure Ruth won't mind,
though?" she asked.

"Ruth? Lord, no! Why should she?" he asked innocently. "She's got Redskin, hasn't she? He's a thoroughbred; she couldn't ask for anything better than he is, I reckon." He put out one hand and tousled her hair a little. "Reckon I got a right to give my kid-sister-in-law a horse, haven't I? Who's got a better right?"

She thrust his hand away and tossed the hair back from her eyes. "O. K., m'lord. . . . By the way, speaking of rights—I guess yours is a mighty one, sure enough, judging by the looks of our range boss! Are you going to tell me now why Mr. Wesley Luckert yearns for your sudden and painful death, Ace?"

"Did he tell you that's what he wanted, imp?"

"Not in so many words, exactly! . . . But—who put the burr in the agent's saddle and sent you down after a registered package that turned out to be nothing but me—and not registered!—and who hired that not-bad-looking murderer to shoot you if it wasn't Wes? Answer me them, if you can!"

"No can do, Kay. All the not-bad-lookin'—says you! he looked right bad to me, at first!—murderer told me about his bein' hired was that he was broke! I got a nice, long expensive wire from the hospital last night sayin' they'd had a devil of a time diggin' the lead out of him, but that he had the constitution of a horse and would probably live in spite of all they could do. Maybe *he'll* turn out to be the 'young Lochinvar from out of the West' you been waitin' for, Kay! Not a bad thing, sometimes, havin' a murderer in the family. Saves hirin' outside talent."

"No young Lochinvar for me, thanks! He was the hombre that rode a snow-white charger, wasn't he? My experience with men on white horses would ruin *his* chances right from the start, thank you! . . . Of course you sent your best gilt-edged check along to pay for the wire and the digging, eh, Ace? You're an awful fool, sometimes; sort of a likeable one, but a fool nevertheless!"

"I sent 'em a check, yes. I'm not sure about it's bein'

very gilt-edged, not havin' failed to dodge my banker in the past few months! But how'd you know that?"

She shrugged. "It's just the sort of thing you'd do, Ace. There come Ruth and Gordon now; someone else, too. Darned if it isn't my paternal ancestor—the chieftain of clan Cameron himself! They must have met him on the road from the Wells!" She left him, running down to meet the approaching riders.

Ace stood up and followed her more closely, his gaze reaching past the running girl to that other who rode so slim and proud between the two tall men. Even at the distance her face, between the two bronzed faces of the men, seemed pale and spiritual; fragile, like the white, patrician features of some fine lady on a cameo.

Steve Cameron swung down from his saddle as they halted at the hitching rack and swept Kay into his arms, his hearty greeting smothered in a bear-like hug. Gordon Wallace dismounted swiftly, too, and Gilbert watched the man's deft courtesy as he helped Ruth down. Cameron was facing the house now, shouting a greeting to Ace as he came up the path, his arm still tight about the waist of his youngest child. There was something oddly similar about those two; a likeness that accounted, possibly, for the deeper love there was between them than between Steve Cameron and Ruth. The Colonel was fiercely proud of his first born; proud of her beauty and her perfect poise. He loved Kay with a rough affection that is usually reserved by a man for his son.

"Howdy, Ace! Good t' see yuh again, son! Reckon yuh're happy now Ruth's back, eh?" He shook Gilbert's hand and poked a sly finger at his ribs. "Been pretty lonesome 'round here this last year, eh? Lord, it's great t' be home again! Home, with both my kids! What d'yuh think o' *this* brat, Ace? She's been tryin' to tell me she's grown up, and she don't even know her own mind yet! Begged me for money t' spend the summer on the coast and then come's tearin' home just when I was anticipatin' a peaceful summer! . . . Come in, boy, and tell me about the cattle business!"

Ruth and Wallace had come up beside them now and

greeted them both smilingly. "Sorry I couldn't get over sooner, Ruth," he said. "Thing's turned up that had to be done, and I couldn't get away."

"Of course, dear. I've been busy, too, showing Gordon that we aren't as wild and woolly as he thought. I believe the man expected Indians on the war-path, and sod shanties, and guns popping all around, and all that! We're convincing him that we're nearly civilized, though, aren't we?"

"Oh, quite civilized, I'm afraid!" Gordon Wallace turned a quizzical smile toward Ace. "I wasn't altogether wrong at that, though. Guns do pop now and then, eh, Gilbert? It's a great country!"

"I think so." Ace fell into step beside him and Ruth laid a hand inside the crook of his arm. Her other hand was on Wallace's sleeve and Ace smiled a little, inwardly, at her calm possessiveness toward both of them. He was not allowed time for further talk, for Steve Cameron turned upon them as they reached the porch, claiming Ace for a talk.

"I've heard nothin' but politics for weeks now, and I want to hear about cows for a change! You let Ace go now, Ruth, and I'll send him back to yuh after a while. My range boss ain't here, so it's up to Ace. I got t' talk t' somebody!"

They made a laughing group for a moment there on the sunlit porch before Gordon Wallace and the two girls accepted their dismissal and left the two cattlemen alone. Cameron watched them go and turned to Ace with a frown.

"Who's this Wallace hombre?" he asked. "Don't know as I approve o' Ruth pickin' up with strangers like that! No tellin' about these foreigners, yuh know. What d'yuh think of him?"

"I reckon you don't need tellin'," Ace told him, grinning. "He's a white man. You can see that. And that's all I know about him. I like him."

"Shucks! So do I! Just wondered how it struck *you,* havin' Ruth gallivantin' around with another man! . . .

Set down, son. What's all this I been hearin' about rus-lin'? Luckert writes me the Triangle is losin' beef."

"I reckon Luckert knows if anybody does, Steve."

"Never liked Wes, did yuh? Well, that's all right, too. How about the Lazy 9? You losin' cows, too?"

"Not yet. All the rustlin' so far has been north of the river. There's been a lot of talk, and some of the boys had a meetin' the other day in town to organize a sort of vigilantes' committee to try to put a stop to the rus-tlin'."

"Makin' yuh the leader, I'll bet a hat!"

"No . . . I didn't attend the meetin', Steve."

"Why not?"

"I haven't lost any cattle—yet."

"That ain't the reason!" Cameron bit the end off a black cigar and his keen eyes never swerved from Gil-bert's face. "Come through, son! I'm listenin'."

"No, that isn't the reason, Steve; not all of it, anyway. I don't believe in these ridin' committees, and I told them so; but—Steve, there's somethin' behind all this that I don't know about! It's nothin' I can lay a finger on, but I've got a hunch that there's a nigger in the wood-pile, somewhere. At least, that's the way I felt then."

"Changed yuhr mind since, Ace?"

"Maybe. If the Lazy 9 starts losin' cattle there'll be a ridin' committee, all right. Only it'll be all Lazy 9 men! I'll back my outfit against any gang of rustlers that ever whirled a loop!"

"Don't blame you. . . . Who's doin' this rustlin', Ace? Yuh know?"

"Buck Wilbur's gang. I didn't believe that, at first; but it's true."

Steve Cameron's hand paused midway in the act of bearing a lighted match to his smoke and hung there for a moment, motionless. His face seemed to stiffen, some-how, as he gazed fixedly at Ace. He carried the match to his smoke finally and puffed the long cigar into the flame with deliberate care before he spoke again. "What makes yuh sure it's—Wilbur?" he asked quietly.

"A man that knew Buck Wilbur in Arizona saw his

gang up in the hills. They killed the man; but before
he died he named the men that got him. I can't tell
you more than that, Steve. It involves people that are
at Wilbur's mercy if it gets out that they told."

"Let me get this straight, Ace." Cameron's shrewd gaze
bored deep as he leaned forward to peer more closely
at Gilbert's face. "Yuh say yuh know Wilbur's doin' the
rustlin'; yuh say this man saw him—or his gang. Yuh
mean—yuh haven't seen—Buck Wilbur yuhrself, have
yuh? Nobody's seen him—except this man he—killed?"

"Not that I know of, Steve. I wouldn't know him if
I did see him. Neither would anyone else around here,
I reckon. But, if you're doubtin' that he's here, I'm
afraid you're makin' a mistake. It sounded fishy to me,
too, at first. But this story about his killin' a man up in
the hills—that's true, Steve. I got it from a source I
can trust; a man that don't talk unless he knows what
he's sayin'. Wilbur's here!"

Steve Cameron blew a streamer of smoke between his
lips and leaned back in his chair again. A certain tension
seemed to have gone out of his face in the last half-
minute, and he sat for a time in silence, breathing
deeply and staring out across the rolling acres that were
his personal domain.

"That's—bad, Ace," he said, finally. "Mighty bad. . . .
Wilbur was a terror down in Arizona a few years back;
hate t' think we're due for the same sort o' thing
here. . . . Wes didn't—tell me—that!"

Ace frowned a little. "Speakin' of Wes, Steve: Wes
and I had a run-in the other day, in town. I've been
hearin' rumors that Wes was hintin' that I knew more
about this rustlin' than was good for me, and the other
night he made the same remark to my face. I reckon
he was sore over losin' cattle here, and took a crack at
me because I haven't been touched. He never liked me,
you know, any more than I've cottoned to him. . . .
Well, we fought it out, and I reckon that didn't prove
much, one way or another. But—somethin's happened
since then that I've got to tell you, Steve; and I hope
you won't think I'm just tryin' to get back at Wes."

"I been knowin' yuh since yuh wore yuhr pants fastened with a safety-pin, Ace. I reckon I won't be accusin' yuh of anything like that!"

"Somebody is goin' too light with his brandin' iron on your calves, Steve. Hair-brandin'. I saw a couple myself, and I don't mind tellin' you I sent my boys up here lookin' for strays, to see how general the habit was. It's pretty bad, Steve. Bad enough so a range boss couldn't very well fail to know. And—Luckert's been hirin' new men here, you know. That makes it look worse. I figured you ought to know."

Cameron's face had hardened again as Gilbert spoke, and his eyes were narrowed to slits. "Yuh mean—yuh're accusin' Wes Luckert o' stealin' my beef, eh, Ace?"

"That's the way it looks, Steve."

Cameron shook his head slowly. "I reckon not, Ace," he said. "Wes wrote me he was havin' the men range-brand each new calf; said he figgered it was the only way to guard against the rustlin'. All the spreads north of the river are doin' it, he said. That's right, ain't it?"

"It may be."

"Of course it is! Unbranded calves are no more'n a temptation to rustlers! Best thing to do if there's a chance o' losin' 'em is to catch 'em and brand 'em on the open range! . . . And I reckon that accounts for what yuh saw. Most punchers nowadays is used to brandin' with a stamp iron; ain't used to a runnin' iron, which they use for range-brandin'. I reckon they ain't got wise to how it's done, yet. 'Nother thing: there's always bound t' be a gold-bricker in an outfit; feller that shirks the hard jobs when he can. Brandin' is damn hard work for one man; I reckon somebody's shirkin' it. I reckon some hombre is ropin' his calf and ear-markin' it and lettin' it up. That'd account for yuhr sleepers, wouldn't it?"

"That'd account for it, sure. Only—one of these calves I saw was wearin' a Triangle brand plain enough when I hazed him back over the river a month or so ago! And there's no brand on him now."

"Goes back to what I said about the boys not understandin' the runnin' iron these days! That is, always supposin' that the sleeper yuh saw was the calf yuh saw wearin' a brand a month or so ago! There's a good many thousand youngsters runnin' around on this range, Ace, and they all look pretty much alike! Easy for a man to make a mistake." He stood up, dropping a friendly hand on Gilbert's shoulder. "Fact is, Ace, I reckon feelin' the way yuh do about Luckert yuh can't help bein' quick t' see somethin' wrong with him. I ain't blamin' yuh, understand; it's natural as hell! But—*Wes Luckert ain't stealin' Triangle stuff, Ace!* Better get that idea out o' yuhr mind!"

# 7 · EDDY LANE

THE EVENING in the Triangle ranch house was pleasant enough, certainly; and yet through it all Ace Gilbert was conscious of a sense of tension in the air. It came from Steve Cameron; was evident in the stern set of his face that was broken only by bursts of over-loud talk or laughter when some direct remark broke through his abstraction. The feeling grew upon Ace as the evening progressed; made him restless and ill at ease.

There was an organ in the spacious living room at the Triangle, and the two girls took turns at drawing plaintive music from its ancient pipes. Now and then its off-key wailing brought bursts of laughter that cut a song in half, but there were times, too, when the four young voices blended sweetly in familiar songs unmarred by organ discord. They danced a little, too, romping through the figures of old square dances in which Gordon Wallace must be taught, or gliding smoothly to the beat of a waltz.

Once, when Ace danced with Kay, the girl tilted her

head far back to meet his eyes in a searching gaze. "What did you say to dad, Ace?" she whispered. "What's wrong?"

He shrugged, noncommittally. "Nothin' wrong, I reckon, imp. What makes you think there is?"

She shook her head without answering, but there were other times, later, when he saw her dark eyes rest questioningly upon her father and then turn accusingly toward himself.

It was good to hold Ruth in his arms again and match steps with her to the slow strains of some old-time waltz. Once during the evening he guided her to the door that led out onto the shadowed porch, and they stepped through for a little while for their first moments alone since her return. She accepted his kiss then, but he had learned restraint since that meeting at the train and he held her lightly, fearing to ask too much.

"You're beautiful, Ruth. If I had known how lonely it would be here without you, I think I wouldn't have let you go!"

"That would have been selfish, Asher; and you aren't that. Oh, it was marvelous, all of it! Seeing all those quaint, beautiful places I'd read about—meeting cultured, interesting people—hearing good music and—all that. I loved it!"

"Didn't you miss me at all, Ruth? Even a little bit?" There was the same wistful hunger in his voice now that had been in it once when he spoke to Kay this afternoon. "Say you love me, Ruth? You do—don't you?"

"Of course I love you, Asher. I missed you, too,—a little!" She laughed at him, gently. "And that's a big compliment, you know; remembering to miss you when I was doing so many pleasant things! . . . We must go in now, dear. We mustn't forget Gordon. . . ."

"I'd be willin' to forget him, for a while!" Ace grumbled, humorously. "I'd be a lot more comfortable about that hombre if I didn't like him so well!"

But they went in, and it was not long after that before Ace made his excuses and began the long ride home. His thoughts turned definitely then upon his talk with Cameron. He had known, of course, that Steve Cameron was partial to the big puncher who bossed the Triangle range, but he had hardly expected such blind allegiance as Cameron had displayed tonight. Had he been wrong in sensing a hint of something that might almost be panic, behind the big man's quick defense of his range boss? There had been some local amusement and talk concerning the quick favor Luckert had found with Cameron when Luckert first came, and it had been justified by the man's swift rise to power over the Triangle range. Cameron liked the man, evidently; or at any rate he trusted him. But even that seemed hardly to account for Cameron's refusal to believe such damning evidence as Ace had shown him now.

Because the evidence *was* damning. A high percentage of "sleepers" on a range could not be overlooked by a range boss, and their presence could mean but one thing; that someone meant to brand them later with a brand of his own. Luckert allowed the condition to exist; hence Luckert must stand to profit thereby. Cameron's suggestion that some Triangle man was shirking work might account for a few such "sleepers," but never for all that were loose on the Triangle range. Then, too, Cameron was too good a cattleman to doubt Ace Gilbert's statement that he had recognized an individual calf. Cattle may look alike to the novice, but to a man like Gilbert each one has distinctive markings, not to be confused. Once his attention was called to a particular animal he would never mistake it. Between men like Cameron and Gilbert, a man's word that he recognized a steer would be accepted as final at the branding pen. So that Cameron's protest now was no more than a subterfuge, and an obvious one. Steve Cameron had been worried and he had seized upon any excuse to defend his foreman. What Gilbert wondered about now was, *why?*

There was a light in the Lazy 9 ranch house when Ace rode into the yard and he had a glimpse through the window of O'Keefe playing solitaire at the table in the living room. The bunkhouse was dark. O'Keefe must have stayed up after the rest of the men had gone to bed; probably to report the findings on the Triangle range. He was still there when Ace returned to the house after unsaddling his horse, but he shoved the cards aside as Ace came in.

"Did yuh happen t' see Eddy today, Ace?" O'Keefe ignored Ace's greeting and put the question with a sharpness that betrayed a worried state of mind.

"No. Anything wrong?"

"Oh, I reckon not. Eddy ain't showed up since he left yesterday mornin', that's all. Cookie said he took the same amount o' grub as the rest of us, so it looks like he'd be driftin' in. Some o' the other boys stayed out over last night, but they all came in tonight."

"Maybe the kid got further away than the others and decided to spend the night at one of the other spreads. I wouldn't worry about him."

"Oh, I'm not worryin', exactly. . . . Stayed up mostly t' see how the Colonel took the news about Wes. Slim said he seen the Colonel ridin' toward home, so I figured yuh'd tell him."

"I told him but I reckon I might just as well not have." Ace sat down at the table facing O'Keefe and related in detail his talk with Cameron. O'Keefe picked up the cards again as Ace talked, dealing them mechanically. He frowned a little and shook his head when Ace stopped speaking.

"I reckon it's hard for the Colonel to believe," he said. "He'll see for himself, though. Give him time."

Ace said nothing, but O'Keefe's natural explanation of Cameron's attitude did not convince him. Cameron's defense of Luckert had been too vehement, somehow; almost as if the Colonel had expected trouble and had determined beforehand to combat it.

O'Keefe spoke again, thoughtfully. "Wonder how come the boys picked Jim Talbert t' lead the vigilantes? Talbert's only been here five-six months. Looks like they'd've picked somebody that knew the range better."

"Talbert's new, all right; but he's sunk a lot of money here, buyin' land and cattle and all. He seems to be a good man, and he's made a lot of friends."

"Yeah. . . . Sort o' goes out o' his way t' make friends, Talbert does." O'Keefe stood up suddenly, listening. "Horse comin' down the trail, Ace; reckon that's Eddy comin' home. I'll roll in now, myself. It's gettin' late."

"Wait!" Gilbert was on his feet now, leaning across the table a bit as he listened to the clip-clop of hoofs that was growing louder now. "That horse is comin' pretty slow, Tim. Not the way the kid always rides . . ."

O'Keefe's reaction was quick and to the point. He had picked up his hat as he spoke before, and he brought it down now in a fanning sweep that snuffed out the light in the table lamp. The sudden darkness engulfed them and Gilbert's startled protest sounded unduly loud. O'Keefe answered in a whisper. "Shut up, damn yuh! Just because they didn't get yuh the first time, down at the station, ain't no reason why yuh should risk a slug through a lighted window! Let's see who this jasper is before we . . ."

But Gilbert had already crossed to the window and was peering out, safe now that the room at his back was dark. There was moonlight in the outer yard and Gilbert saw the horseman as he came into view around the bunkhouse. He laughed a little. "It's the kid, all right. Looks like he was takin' a cat-nap in the saddle! . . . No, by—God!" His voice changed sharply on the last word and he whirled to the door, jerking it open and darting out.

O'Keefe lunged after him, shouting a question. Gilbert's voice came back, tensely: "He fell! Somethin's wrong, Tim! The kid's hurt!"

They crossed the yard at a headlong run toward the horse standing now with an empty saddle, head lowered toward the huddled figure on the ground. The boy was sobbing softly as Gilbert bent over him, but the sobs ceased as Ace spoke his name.

"Eddy! Good God, boy what's happened?"

"Ace? . . . Ace, it's yuh, ain't it? . . . Don't lift me. I'm all shot to hell! . . . But I wasn't cryin' because I'm hurt, Ace. I didn't know I was—home, and I was cryin'—because I knew I couldn't get back—in the saddle again."

"It's all right, son. You're home. What happened?" Gilbert's voice was low and strained. Eddy Lane had told the truth about his condition. His body was riddled. His clothes were so soaked with blood it seemed impossible that he could have lost so much and remained alive.

"Rustlers, Ace. . . . I was—comin' home and bumped right into 'em at the ford west o' the old corral. They— cut loose before I—knew what was up, Ace. I tried—t' get my gun out, but—things went all black. I'm sorry— I couldn't stop 'em. . . ."

"Forget it, Ed." Ace spoke gruffly, fighting the lump in his throat. "We'll get 'em for you, son! You did a man-sized job to bring the news."

"Yuh—mean that, Ace? . . . And yuh mean—yuh'll go after 'em?" Ace nodded, fearing to trust his voice. "Gosh! I wish—I could ride with yuh, Ace! I always—knew yuh'd be a—fightin' fool if yuh ever—started. Tim says —yuh're lightnin' fast—on the draw. . . . I wish yuh'd tell the boys I—died game, will yuh, Ace? . . . I . . ." His voice drifted off into nothingness and Ace felt his body stiffen in the last gallant fight before the end. It was some time before Ace Gilbert stood erect again, and when he did there were tears on his cheeks which he did not trouble to brush away.

O'Keefe's eyes were wet, too; and there were three or four sleepy-eyed punchers back of him, attracted from the bunkhouse by the noise outside. They carried Eddy's body on a blanket to the house and laid him gently on a bed for the last and longest sleep. Outside in the big living room once more, Tim O'Keefe spoke for the first time since he had left it with Ace a while ago.

"I don't see how he ever got home," he said. "It must've been—hell—gettin' into a saddle, cut to pieces like he was. . . . I hope I'm as game as he was, when it comes my time t' go!"

The room was filled now with solemn, stricken men. Every man from the Lazy 9 bunkhouse was there now and each one waited for Gilbert to speak. There was a long, sad silence. Ace stood at a window, staring out across the moonlit yard. He turned at last, avoiding the eyes that searched his face.

"Better get back and try to get some sleep, boys," he said. "I'll sit up with—him. . . . We can't do anything in the dark. I'll call you in time to hit the west ford by dawn. If you can't sleep. . . ." His voice hardened perceptibly now. "If you can't sleep, you might spend the time oilin' up your guns! The Lazy 9 is declarin' war! If anybody's got any objections to fightin', now'd be a real good time for him to draw his time!"

Tim O'Keefe growled an answer for them all. "Yuh can't get rid of us *that* easy, Ace! Yuh just call the dance an' by God, we'll play the music!"

Ace nodded. "I knew that," he said. "All right. Tim, go tell Cookie to start throwin' food together; sandwiches —stuff we can carry; eight men, for two days. Send Squint for the saddle string. The rest of you, take that deck and deal the cards once around. First spade goes to town to report Eddy's death to Sheriff Robertson. Next four spades will stay here."

They dealt the cards and there was some low-voiced profanity over the decision they proclaimed. The men filed out then, one by one, the muffled sound of their steps fading in the distance as they returned to the bunkhouse. Ace Gilbert had returned to the window to stand staring out across the moonlit yard. A light flickered weakly and then grew steady and strong in the bunkhouse. The men were not in a mood for sleep, then. Well, neither was he! But they'd all need it, perhaps; there might be little sleep for any of them if they struck a warm trail in the morning. But the necessity for inaction irked him and he turned restlessly to find Tim O'Keefe in the room again. "You better try to sleep, Tim," he said tonelessly.

"What's the use?" Tim answered without meeting Gilbert's eyes. Ace was glad of that, and he understood. Neither of them cared to display the emotion that must be plain in each pair of eyes. "Wish we could ride now.

Them hombres'll push the cattle hard tonight; have a long start."

"You can't read trail in the dark, Tim. We'll save time by waitin'."

And so they waited, their silence a tribute to the boy who had died game, and a grim prelude to the ride that would avenge his death. The hours passed monotonously, each one ten times its length in the minds of the waiting men. It was four o'clock when Ace rose stiffly from his chair and met O'Keefe's inquiring glance. He nodded.

"Tell 'em to saddle, Tim. Get the roan for me; no use takin' the risk of gettin' Satan hurt."

They mounted in a chill dark that precedes the dawn, warmed and livened a little by the steaming stirrup-cup that had been the cook's contribution to revenge, but still grim and tight-lipped and silent. They rode swiftly while the east turned grey behind them, each man bent forward a little in an eagerness that made their pace seem slow.

It was dawn when they reached the ford west of the old branding corral, and they paused there for a moment to read the sign in the dust. Many cattle had crossed there in the night, driven northward by mounted men; fifty cattle and four men, according to O'Keefe's reading of the sign. Yonder, a little north of the ford, they found a dark stain and the twisted prints of a man's body on the ground; a man who had crawled, later, inch by inch, a hundred yards or more to a spot where he had pulled himself up beside the clustered hoof-marks of a horse. They read those signs grimly, seeing in them the heroic story of a boy's stubborn fight with death out of loyalty to his friends.

The trail of the cattle led northward still and they followed it, reading from the tracks the proof of urgent haste. The shooting at the ford must have taken place about nightfall, Ace thought. Some time must have elapsed before Eddy Lane had regained consciousness, and it would have taken hours for a man so wounded to reach his horse and mount and make the ride to the Lazy 9. That timing, too, would agree with the logical scheme of the rustlers. They would have planned to start their drive as soon as darkness fell in order to give themselves as much time as possible for the long drive to the hills. For there was no doubt in his mind that this trail would lead them into the Mescalero range. That, almost certainly, was Buck Wilbur's stronghold, and there alone would they find a hiding place for stolen stock.

Two hours brought them to the crest of the high bluffs that rimmed the valley on the north and marked the beginning of the Mescalero foothills. Westward, five miles or more, Jim Talbert's Rocking M ranch house nestled in a fold of the rolling prairie land in which it stood. Far to the east lay Joseph "Tubby" Martin's JM range. Beyond that Lyle Long's Double L cattle grazed the rich slopes where the Mescaleros swung back sharply to double the width of Thunder River valley. And to the northward, tall now with nearness, were the hills themselves . . .

Ace drew rein sharply as they topped the crest and sat silent, staring at a mile-wide strip of smoking, blackened land that lay ahead. Tim O'Keefe pulled up beside him and swore. "They fired the range, the ——'s!" he said. "Burned out their trail, so we couldn't tell where they hit the hills!"

Gilbert nodded. "Smart trick," he said. "The burn runs northeast across the trail we've been followin' so far. Wind was from the southwest last night, so they must have left a man behind to set the fire after they'd driven the cattle on. . . . Funny they went so far downwind to start it; the burn runs that way as far as I can see; must have been set somewhere near Talbert's place."

O'Keefe shrugged. "It might've run back a good deal from where it was set," he said. "Wind was gentle all night. . . . This won't stop us, though. Only thing is, we'll have to cover the whole front of the burn where it hits the hills to find where they went in. Let's go, eh? Might as well get at it."

The pace was even faster now that there was no need of hunting sign. The broad, still-smouldering track of the fire was an unmistakable highway and they spurted forward to gain if they could a part of the time they would lose later on. Where the Mescaleros reared their first ramparts out of the lesser hills Ace Gilbert halted his men and outlined his plan.

"Spread out and follow every canyon in until you find where the fire stopped. Look beyond that for traces of cattle. If you find sign, ride back to the mouth of the canyon and fire a shot. Better keep your eyes peeled, because they may have left men to guard their trail. Use your judgment. That's all. But—I aim to hunt every pocket in these hills until we find what we're after! . . . Get goin'!"

They whirled their mounts and Ace raised his voice sharply to halt them again. "By the way, Tim: I told Kay Cameron she could have that pinto gelding—Satan's colt, you know—for a saddle mount. If anything happens to me, see that she gets it, will you?"

"O. K., Ace. But—if yuh let anything happen t' yuh, I'll break yuhr damn neck! That stuff about keepin' yuhr eyes peeled goes for yuh, too!"

It was odd that he should have thought of that promise to Kay, now. Ace wondered about that, vaguely, as he entered the canyon that was his to search. Been more natural, he thought, if he had sent some message to Ruth in case things went wrong with him. Funny how a man's mind works, sometimes. . . .

# 8 · KIDNAPPED

KAY CAMERON retired very soon after Ace Gilbert left the Triangle on the night of his first visit since her return. Ruth and Gordon Wallace had remained on the porch after Ace's departure and the low murmur of their voices came up to Kay's ears like the sleepy drone of bees. Steve Cameron had gone to his room, but evidently he had not found sleep imperative, for Kay could hear the steady tramp of his feet in the room beneath her own.

It was not these things, however, that kept her awake. It was her own thoughts that kept her eyes wide in the velvety darkness and she lay very still, sending her mind back through the events of the day. It was good to be home. She smiled a little in the dark, and put the thought into words, silently. "Hypocrite!" she called herself. "You mean it's good to be where there's a chance of seeing Ace once in a while! . . . He wasn't so darned eager to see Ruth, apparently, or he'd have come before today. . . . Well, I played fair with her—or tried to. I told him how I'd want him to make love to me, anyway. I wonder if he'll try it? If he did—if he wouldn't *respect* her so much—if he'd jar her out of her dignified pose a little and make her love him . . . oh, *damn!* There wouldn't be any chance for me, *then;* that's sure! But there isn't anyway. She's so pretty, and he's been crazy about her since we were kids. . . ."

But there were other memories—other thoughts less barbed than these—that crowded in. There was the haunting note of wistfulness in Ace's voice as he said, "Yes, you *would* want—that." She had just told him the kind of a lover she would want her lover to be. . . . "But Ruth doesn't," he had added, regretfully, or had she only imagined the regret? And later . . . "Nobody'd want you to be like anybody but you. You're pretty sweet as you are, you know." And then he had spoiled it by switching instantly to talk of Ruth, as if he had been thinking of her even as he spoke!

Ruth and Gordon came inside at last and Kay heard Ruth come up the stairs and go into her room further down the hall. Gordon had the bedroom on the first floor, beside Steve Cameron's room, and she heard his door close softly and later the protesting squeak as he pulled his window up. Steve Cameron was still awake, for she could hear him moving restlessly about beneath her. He had been restless and ill at ease all evening, she recalled. Something Ace had said to him must have worried him. She wondered what that something could have been; and then, gradually, she drifted off into sleep.

It was just dawn when she was awakened reluctantly to the sound of many hoofs in the yard. A door opened somewhere downstairs and boots thumped briefly on the porch. Then her father's voice, curt and compelling: "Wes! I want t' talk t' yuh!" The boots thumped again on the porch and the door opened and shut. Other boots, later; and another opening and closing of a door. She dozed again for a little while, but the voices in the room downstairs pounded against her consciousness and drove sleep away. She threw the covers back and greeted the day dubiously. Her window was wide open and directly over the one in her father's room, which must also be open, judging by the noise. She hoped they weren't waking Gordon. He was used to late rising, she supposed. Luckily his window was on the other side of the house. Why must they talk so loudly, anyway?

She walked to the window and the voices came more clearly. Her father's voice first, thick with anger: "Yuh lied t' me, Wes! Tricked me into a mess that'll ruin me if it's known! Damn yuh, ain't there a spark o' decency in yuh anywhere?"

Then Luckert's voice, growling and defiant: "Lay off preachin', Steve! It makes me sick! Who told yuh this stuff, anyhow? Who's been here?" A pause; then Luckert again: "Gilbert, wasn't it? Come up t' make calf-eyes at Ruth and spilled a lot o' lies t' yuh. . . ."

"They ain't lies, Wes! Ace wouldn't say a thing like that unless he was damned sure. . . ."

"It *was* Gilbert then! Well, by God, it's the last time he'll stick his nose into my business! You've signed a death warrant fer that precious son-in-law o' yuhrs, *sabe*? From now on, my men—all of 'em!—will be out t' get him! Yuh know what *that* means, don't yuh?" Luckert's harsh laughter drifted up and Kay shuddered, not with cold.

"Yuh can't do that, Wes!" For once Kay Cameron

heard a note that was almost pleading in the voice of her father! But it was short-lived. His next words were curt; defiant. "If yuh lay a finger on Ace, I, personally, will lead every man the Triangle hires t' hunt you down, Wes! I'll put the law on yuhr trail, no matter what it costs me, too!"

"T' hell with the law! It's never bothered me, for long, has it? And yuh'll lead the Triangle men to hunt me down, eh, Steve? That's rich! Why man, yuh'll only have one man left on this spread when I leave! Tony—yuhr half-witted wrangler! The rest of 'em are *my* men—*sabe?* I hired 'em—the old outfit, you understand? And they'll come with me. I'm through with the Triangle anyway; was fixin' to leave already. Workin' here was fine for me while I got the boys together. They're here now, and I don't need yuh! Yuh didn't think I'd be content to nurse cows for the rest of my life, did yuh? . . . So long, Steve, yuh'll be hearing from me—*soon!*"

The door slammed again, and boots thumped once more on the planking of the porch. Kay drew back from the window, peeping past its frame to watch Luckert stride off in the direction of the barns. He walked cockily, light on his feet, and one loosely clenched fist beat a tattoo against his thigh as he moved. She saw him gather the men about him and talk to them a moment; saw them turn to finish the tasks of unsaddling which they had begun, only to rope out new mounts from the corral and saddle again. Evidently Luckert's boast had been a true one. The Triangle men were *his* men; were leaving with him.

But what did it all mean? Kay tried desperately to fit together the bits of the puzzle in her mind even while she dressed, but the answer would not come. What strange hold had Luckert over her father? What had Ace Gilbert to do with it? Luckert's threat regarding Ace was no idle one, she knew. Luckert's voice, sneering, throaty, packed with menace, had told her that; and she knew the man well enough to know that he would make it good if the opportunity ever came. She jerked riding boots over her slim feet, ran a comb through her hair hastily, and pulled her hat down to hide its disarray. A thunder of hoofs in the yard told her that Luckert and the men were leaving, but she did not look outside. She ran downstairs and to her father's room; almost collided with him in the open door.

"Dad! What is it? Where are you going?" She took in at a glance the rigid set of his face, eyes narrowed, jaw clenched so that the cords in his cheek stood out; saw the heavy gun strapped at his hip and remembered oddly that she had not seen him armed since the day he had gone out to kill a colt that had cut himself horribly in barbed wire. That was more than a year ago. . . .

"Get back t' bed, honey. I'll tend t' this, all right. It ain't nothin' for yuh t' worry yuhr head about."

"But, Dad! I heard—heard Wes Luckert say he would kill Ace! What *is* it, Dad? You've got to tell me!"

But he brushed her aside almost roughly, refusing to speak. Something made him pause then and turn, swinging her around and into his arms. He kissed her gently and pushed her away again; whirled and almost ran through the outer door and across the porch.

She followed at his heels, and saw him mount a horse that stood waiting for him at the rack. He must have ordered it before his talk with Luckert, she thought. The horse snorted wildly as Cameron's spurs struck deep; lunged away and into racing stride in a frenzy of fear and pain. That sight alone would have told Kay the seriousness of the affair. Steve Cameron loved horses, and the one he rode today was his special pet.

She found Tony at the corral and made him rope and saddle a mount for her. "Not Spotty; get me that buckskin there; and hurry, Tony! Please hurry!"

Tony hurried, but the moments spent in catching and saddling the horse seemed endless to Kay and once she was in the saddle she sent the buckskin at a relentless speed toward the south and the Lazy 9. She had no idea where her father had gone; whether he had ridden to warn Ace himself or not. The possibility that he had not was enough. She would see to it that Ace had his warning, provided she could reach him in time. The thought was in her mind that Wes Luckert might lead his men directly to the Lazy 9 for an immediate attack and from each bit of higher ground she searched the trail for the dust that might betray other horsemen ahead of her. Once or twice she did see dust, but it seemed to her that it was not enough to indicate a large body of men. Perhaps it was her dad . . .

The buckskin was heavily lathered when she drew rein at last at the Lazy 9 and she flung down from the saddle and ran to the door of the main house. Her knocks brought no answer. A voice from the bunkhouse called her name and she turned to meet Squint Jenkins, sleepy-eyed from a nap, but curious.

"Where's Ace, Squint? I've got to find him—quick!"

"He's gone, Miss Kay; left 'fore day, this mornin'. Yuh see, somebody killed Eddy Lane last night, and Ace is out lookin' for 'em."

"Poor Eddy! I'm certainly sorry to hear it. But—where is Ace looking? I'll find him . . ."

"Reckon yuh couldn't do that, Miss Kay. They'd be ridin' right fast, I expect. Yuhr dad was here just a few minutes ago lookin' for Ace, and he started out t' try catchin' him, too. Yuh see, Eddy was killed at the ford out west o' the brandin' corral; so they'd have t' pick up the trail there, but where they'd go from there is a gamble. They'd be followin' the trail them rustlers left, yuh see?"

"They? Then Ace isn't alone?"

Squint grinned. "Not exactly!" he said. "They was seven mighty mad boys with him when he left here!"

"That's something, at least! It was rustlers that killed Eddy, you say? And I suppose Dad would go to the ford to pick up their trail."

"That's what he said he'd do, Miss Kay. But I told him I reckoned it wa'n't no use."

"Thanks, Squint." Kay left the man gaping as she whirled and ran to her horse again. If it had been rustlers who had killed Eddy Lane, it seemed to her a certainty that their trail would lead straight to the Mescalero hills, and in that case Ace and his men would ride that way.

Her father had gone to the ford to take up the trail at its beginning; but that meant riding two sides of a great triangle, and a stern chase at best. If she cut through from the Lazy 9 she would be riding one side of the triangle with a chance of intercepting Ace before he entered the hills. It was a long gamble, at best; but she took it without hesitation.

The buckskin was game enough, but it was evident very soon that he was tired. She had ridden thoughtlessly, setting a killing pace to the Lazy 9 because she had hoped that her quest would end there. If she had known from the start that it was to be an endurance test she could have saved the horse and warmed him gradually to his task. But she could not spare him, now, certainly. Squint was right in supposing that Ace and his men would ride hard, once they had struck the trail. They, too, would be facing a stern chase and would try to make up lost time.

She chose her trail carefully once she had crossed the river again, keeping as much as possible to the ridges from which she could see the country on either side. But, in spite of her haste, the morning was half gone before she had reached the bluffs that marked the northern boundary of Triangle range and so far she had seen no sign of the Lazy 9 posse. The buckskin was staggering when they reached the end of the climb up the bluff and Kay dismounted for a time to give him a breathing spell. She had never entered the foothills at just this point before and the delay would give her time to orient herself. The country was rougher here than she had remembered it, and she weighed the advisability of swinging more to the west in the hope of finding easier going there. She turned that way, leading the buckskin along a steep defile that angled westward and up to the higher ground where a foothill ridge came down to form a jagged crest along the bluff itself.

A spurt of smoke shot up from the ridge ahead as she faced that way, and Kay halted in the shadow of a jutting ledge to watch. Other spurts followed the first, spaced in changing rhythm: two quick puffs, a pause, then three; a longer pause, then two quick puffs again, and then three more. She waited, tensely. It was a signal, of course; but who would be making smoke-talk here? Not Ace, certainly. The rustlers, perhaps? It must be that! She reasoned the thing out in her mind as she pulled the buckskin back around a twist in the arroyo and tied him there. They must have known that they were being pursued, and had gone to ground to let the pursuit go by. Perhaps the signals were broadcasting the position of Ace and his men. Perhaps the lookout up there could see them, even now. . . .

She crept past the protecting shoulder of rock and moved stealthily up toward the spot from which the smoke had come. A man stood up for a moment, sil-houetted against the sky, and Kay crouched like a rabbit behind a rock, fearing that she had been seen. But the man was staring toward the west, instead. He turned finally and came toward Kay; dropped out of sight into some deeper crevice that must lie between her and the summit. She breathed again, and continued her stalk. Voices came to her now, low and broken. Once a pebble turned under her foot and she crouched for a long time, rigid with fear of discovery. But there was no change in the drone of those voices ahead, and she went on again. The crevice in which she moved deepened gradually and twisted sharply to the left. And as she neared the angle the sound of the voice became increasingly clear.

She reached the shoulder finally and peeped past it furtively. The arroyo ended just ahead of her present hiding place, opening into a larger niche. And there were men there! Many men—a dozen or more, she thought, although not all were visible from her vantage point.

A voice reached her clearly now: "He come into sight just as I started sendin'. He'll be here in a minute. Must o' been tyin' his hoss when I went up to the ridge."

"It's about time!" This voice, surly and resonant, Kay knew instantly! It was Luckert! The realization left her gasping for a moment. Blind luck had brought her into contact with the very man whose aim she was striving to defeat! Or was it luck? She had been seeking Ace; had come the way Ace must have gone. Perhaps Luckert was hunting Ace, too. Perhaps she had stumbled on an ambush! Her mind raced with the possibilities of the discovery she had made, and for a time she lost the sequence of the talk coming to her past the shoulder of the rock.

When she looked again there was a new figure within the range of her sight; a man whose face was plain to her in profile, although she did not know him. There were gruff greetings, and Luckert's voice again: "Yuh took a long time gettin' here! It's been two hours since we signalled the first time."

The newcomer spoke now. "How was I t' know yuh'd be signallin' today? Lucky t've seen yuh at all! I wouldn't have if I hadn't been watchin' Gilbert through the glass!"

"Gilbert?" Luckert's tone was eager now. "Did he head for the hills?"

"Sure! The fire fooled him. I waited till he was out o' sight before I started. I knew he'd be hot on the trail when yuh told me about downin' that kid at the ford."

"I reckon yuh think we should've let the kid high-tail it to Gilbert last night and have him catch us on the open range, eh?" Luckert's laughter was sneering. "Well, we didn't! . . . I got news for yuh, Jim. The play-actin' is over with, *sabe?* Gilbert snooped and seen some sleepers on the Triangle, and spilled it to Steve. Steve and me had a run-in this mornin', and I'm through. Me and the boys pulled out, pronto. From now on, we'll work it just like we did in the old days, see? I was gettin' tired o' this two-bit business, anyway. Now, we'll make a cleanin', quick!"

The man called Jim cut in, fearfully. "Yuh didn't tell Cameron about *me,* did yuh?"

Luckert chuckled. "I ain't a damn fool, am I? All Steve knows is that his idea o' reformin' me didn't take! Yuh're my ace in the hole, yuh know! I wouldn't give my hand away by tellin' Steve about *yuh,* would I?"

"Well, I hope not! But, look here, man! Steve Cameron

is sure to talk, ain't he? He'll figger it's his duty t' tell the world about yuh, won't he?"

"Well, what if he does? Everybody knew about me before, didn't they? And we got along!"

"Yes, but how about that business on the fifteenth, Wes? That means a fat haul, and we need it right now, believe me! I've got to meet the notes on the ranch, and the cattle we've got won't be safe to sell for a couple of weeks, at least. And the job depends on yuhr bein' able to get into White's office. If the whole country knows who yuh are, yuh'll strike trouble the minute yuh hit the Wells, and the whole thing'll be off!"

"Hell! I never thought o' that. But—I don't really think Steve'll talk. Anyway he tells it, he's in it pretty deep himself and he'll think twice before he ruins himself up at Salt Lake! He said he'd talk, sure, if I did what I said I'd do to Gilbert; and I reckon he would, in that case. But I can't afford t' settle with Gilbert till this other thing is off, anyway. No; as long as I don't touch that damn future son-in-law o' his, I think Steve'll keep mum!"

The other man nodded slowly. He wore a beard, and the stiff point of it under his chin made his profile a thing of sharp angles, unforgettable. "It'd ruin him politically, all right, if the truth came out. But I hate takin' a chance on it. Best thing t' do would be t' shut his mouth, seems t' me."

Luckert spoke again, after a pause. "No, Jim, I draw the line there. Damned if I'll see Steve killed, if that's what yuh mean. I get sore enough t' do it, sometimes, but—he's been pretty white t' me."

"Wouldn't be necessary t' go that far, I reckon. But it'd be a damn sight safer if he could be kept from seein' anybody until after the fifteenth! As yuh say, once *that* job is done, the cat'll be out o' the bag, anyway. It wouldn't matter how much he talked after that."

"Well, suppose I take the boys and surround the Triangle, then. Steve's sure to take a ride some time t'day, if only t' get the feel of a horse under him again. We could pick him up and hold him prisoner until after the fifteenth and then turn him loose!"

"Good! Do that, then! And yuh better get goin', fore he gives yuh the slip and gets t' town! . . ."

There was more, but Kay dared not stay to hear. She had no idea which course Luckert and his men would take from their rendezvous, and if they came this way they would be certain to discover her. She crept back down the arroyo, more swiftly now, until she reached her horse; led him back along the rim of the bluff to the spot where she had made her ascent. The buckskin was stronger now, having rested; but Kay noted approvingly that he had not cooled off enough to become stiff. If she kept him moving now he would cool gradually and be none the worse for his day's work.

She had chosen the ridges before, but now she reversed her preference and sought the lower, less conspicuous course. Not until she was a mile or more from the base of the bluff did she dare expose herself even for a moment against the skyline, and then she risked it only because the ridge lay between herself and the course on which Steve Cameron would be trailing Ace.

She saw him instantly as she came up upon the summit of the ridge; a lone horseman forging doggedly northward to protect a friend at his own cost. And at the same time, Kay saw a close-packed group of riders silhouetted against the sky at the top of the bluff. Luckert's men! They milled there for a moment and then came over the rim in a sliding, precarious descent that veiled them in a cloud of dust.

It could mean but one thing. Luckert had seen Cameron and was bent now upon making the capture he had planned. Fate was playing into Luckert's hands now, as it had played into Kay's hands a little while ago. And there was nothing that Kay could do! Steve Cameron was a mile, at least, from where she stood; less than half of that from the bluff and Luckert. It was as if she occupied a gallery seat at a play in which she had no part.

She saw her father rein up as he caught sight of the men who came toward him; saw Luckert's riders close in. There was a moment of inaction, while they talked; then a flurry as Luckert's men smothered Cameron's resistance by the weight of their numbers. The group separated again in a moment, and then moved slowly back toward the bluff. Kay could distinguish her father again, and knew that he must be disarmed or even bound. Her first instinct was to follow them; but she dared not until they had passed from sight, and in that period of inaction she had time to reason out her course.

"It's up to me, now," she told herself. "Up to me to warn Ace, and all that. If they caught me, too, there'd be nobody . . . and if they saw me and I had to run, my horse would last about a mile! They aren't going to *hurt* dad, after all; and . . . oh, damn! I wish Ace were here! He'd know what to do."

But she decided wisely, after all; decided to return to the Triangle and place the problem in stronger hands. The Triangle lay almost directly east of her now, and she turned the buckskin that way, allowing him to choose his own gait in spite of her own almost irresistible desire for haste.

It was noon when she reached home again, and she went at once to Gordon Wallace. "It's a shame to drag you into family troubles," she told him; "but I'm desperate, and you're just elected, that's all!"

She told him of the talk she had overheard that morning between her father and Luckert, and of her ride to the Lazy 9 and beyond. She told, too, of the rendezvous she had discovered on the bluff; of the talk she had heard, and of her father's capture by Luckert's men. When she had done, Wallace took her hand in one of his and patted it gently.

"Tryin' day, what? Mind if I say you're a confoundedly surprising girl? Gilbert's a lucky chap to have such friends. Fond of him, aren't you?" His shrewd eyes softened understandingly as the girl nodded, turning her face away. He patted her hand again and stood up quickly. "Now, to business, eh? Stop me if I go wrong, won't you? Friend Gilbert is off in the hills with the unpronounceable name, hunting cattle thieves. He won't find 'em, the fact being that the man Luckert is the thief and he is not in the hills. So Gilbert will be back, eh? Maybe soon, maybe not. This is the tenth, and Mr. Luckert is planning his little party, whatever it may be, for the fifteenth. Gilbert should be back by then, no? Oughtn't to take that long to find he's off the scent. . . . Right! Now, Colonel Cameron is to be held prisoner to prevent him from spoiling Mr. Luckert's little game, but he isn't to be hurt. I wonder, by the way, why Mr. Luckert turned scrupulous about that, eh? Not like him. Young man at the ford was in his way; got shot down. Colonel Cameron is in his way, too; but no shooting! . . . Any ideas about this thing on the fifteenth?"

"Yes. They mentioned having to get into White's office, you know. That must mean the bank at Wells. Mr. White is president of the bank."

"Right! The bank it is! Fits in, doesn't it? Bit by bit. All right. Now we have the choice of telling the whole tale to Scotland Yard, or not. Somehow or other, telling is apt to hurt your father, eh? Mustn't feel badly about that, you know. Lots of men get in jams through no fault of their own. Innocent enough business, ten to one; but it would look bad, politically, or at least friend Luckert thinks it would. Safest thing is to suppose Luckert is right, no? Then we'd be muffing it if *we* told! Right? Here's a thought: We keep still at least until friend Gilbert comes home, eh? Tell Gilbert, and let him decide. Likely he knows enough about the situation to know what to do; whereas we'd be going it blind. Sound reasonable to you?"

"Yes . . . yes, I think so. Oh, Ace will surely see some way out of it! Yes, let's wait for him! And thanks a lot, Gordon. You're—darned comforting, anyway!"

She left him then, and Gordon Wallace stood for a long time, staring at the door through which she had gone. "By George!" he said at last. "Hope I didn't muff it too badly! Not heroic, at all; no! But I'd put my foot in it certainly if I jumped at it. Seemed to be a time for conservative watch-and-waiting, if I'm a judge!" And then, still later: "Spunky girl, that! And fond of friend Gilbert . . . by George! Rotten break for us both, his loving Ruth instead!"

# 9 • RED CURTIS

It was a gaunt, weary, disheartened crew that rode down out of the Mescalero hills three days later to begin the homeward march. Horses and men alike showed the rigors of the long, hard trail with little rest and scanty food. They were tired, and their bodies were saddle-sore, and the minds of the men were dulled with the bitterness and disappointment and defeat. For three days, and for the better part of two long nights as well, they had combed the hills for traces of the men they sought; had stood watch on the peaks at night for the glimmer of a fire that might betray the quarry; had ridden always with nerves taut and strained in the fear that every rock and turning might disclose an ambush. And they had found nothing. Here and there among the canyons they had seen cattle—strays from the various ranchs, as wild and sure-footed, seemingly, as mountain goats; and once they had gathered at the cabin of O'Keefe's friends, the Fergusons, where the girl, Mary, had given them food and hot coffee while they heard from her father that he had seen nothing that would aid their search and that he had no further indication of Buck Wilbur's presence in the hills.

"I reckon old Ferguson was right," O'Keefe said now as they followed the black trail of the fire southward. "I'd bet there ain't a rattlesnake in the Mescaleros that I wouldn't recognize by ear after this! If there's rustlers in there, they must be dead and buried and their graves forgot! We searched every pocket within twenty miles of anywhere, and there ain't no place a man could drive

77

cattle that we didn't go. What's next, Ace? Far as I'm concerned, I'm stumped!"

Ace shook his head wearily. "There's an idea floatin' around in my mind, Tim; but it's pretty vague. Even if it were right, I don't quite see how it'd fit in. . . . Wish you'd mill around in your mind, Tim, and see if you can figure out any brand that would blot most of the ones used in the valley. Take mine, and the Triangle, and the JM, and the Double L, and Hitchcock's T Down —that's most of the big ones. See if you can work out a brand that would cover 'em all, sabe? It'll give you somethin' to think about, anyway."

They reached the Lazy 9 by mid-morning and Ace found bewildering news awaiting him. Squint Jenkins, horse-wrangler for the Lazy 9, was the first man he saw and Squint spouted words before Ace had had time to more than dismount.

"Colonel Cameron was here t' see yuh, Ace, the mornin' yuh went away. Tore right out, hopin' t' catch up with yuh. He'd just left when Miss Kay rode in. She sure must've been wantin' t' see yuh mighty bad, too; cause her horse was plumb staggerin', she'd rode him so hard! Then this mornin' early they was another jasper blew in askin' for yuh; a stranger, this was. Sort of a puny lookin' feller, like he'd been sick or somethin'. Said yuh'd remember him; said he met yuh at the station south o' Wells. He give me a letter for yuh; said he'd wait t' see yuh if he could, but somethin' might happen, and if anythin' did happen I was t' be sure t' hold on t' the letter and see yuh got it. Well, I sent him t' the bunkhouse and was tendin' the horses when one o' the Triangle fellers rode in and went straight t' the bunkhouse. Time I could get there, this first hombre and the Triangle man was gettin' on their hosses and pullin' out. Tex Masters, the Triangle man was. Just as they was leavin', the sick-lookin' one grinned at me and said, 'Well, it's happened! So long!' Masters didn't say nothin', but I looked at 'em both right close and, Ace, the sick hombre didn't have no gun in his holster! I knew he had one when he first rode in, 'cause it was pearl-handled and I noticed it, special. What yuh reckon? . . ."

"Where's the letter, Squint?" Ace cut in, curtly.

"Right here inside my shirt!" Squint fumbled mysteriously in his clothing for a moment and produced a soiled envelope. Ace took it and ripped it open. There was no date, nor any salutation:

"You was right about Luckert hirin' me. Only his name aint Luckert. Down in Arizona they used to call him Wes Farley—One-shot Farley. But I reckon that aint his name either. He was Buck Wilbur's right hand man down there. Wilbur's dead, aint many as knows it though. Wes collected the old gang and is trying to take Wilbur's place. I dont make a practice of dry-gulching men, but Luckert had the goods on me over a deal down south, and I was broke. First time I ever squealed on a man, either; but you was real white to me. Reckon I'd a died sure if you hadnt done what you did. While I'm telling it I might as well tell all I know, which aint much because I just hit Utah the day we met. But I judge from the talk that Luckert is rustling and turning the beef over to somebody there whose brand blots all the others in the country, or most of them. Don't know which brand it is, but maybe you can figger it. A feller seen me get off the train and has follered me, so I'm writing this on the chance I won't get to see you. I gave him the slip out of town, but I'm still weak and cant ride long without stopping to rest, so he'll likely catch me. So long, and much obliged."

The letter was signed "Red Curtis."

Gilbert's face was very stern when he turned to Squint again, but he laid a friendly hand on the wrangler's arm. "You did well, Squint. . . . I reckon the sickly lookin' man is—over his sickness, now. I reckon he's—dead! . . . Jerk the saddle off the roan for me, Squint; and saddle Satan. Tim, I hate to do it when the boys are needin' rest so bad; but I think we'd better ride up to the Triangle. Must be somethin' important's happened to bring Steve and Kay both down here; and Kay's too good a hand with a horse to ride one down the way Squint said unless somethin' was wrong. Squint, you get fresh horses for all the boys. I want to talk to Tim."

Squint nodded and left at a run. Ace walked slowly to the bunkhouse and squatted down with his back against the wall. "You figured out the brand I was askin' you about yet, Tim?"

"I reckon not. I can put most of 'em together, all right; but yuh try workin' the JM and the LL, for instance, into the same brand and yuh got a job!"

"It can be done, though. . . . Suppose I was to tell you I knew where those cattle went? The ones we were lookin' for in the hills?"

"I'd say, why the hell didn't yuh go there, if yuh know, instead o' prowlin' around in them mountains?"

Ace grinned. "I didn't see it in time, Tim. Look!" He picked up a bit of weedstem from the ground and began making patterns in the dust. "Here's the main brands used on Thunder River. First, the Triangle: △ Then Tubby Martin's JM, made like this: ⋀⋀ . Then Lyle Long's Double L: ⫽ . Then there's Tommy Hitchcock's T Down: ⊥ . And there's the Lazy 9: ⌐⌐ . Now, suppose I hit this country and started a spread, aimin' to stock my range by means of a wide loop and a runnin' iron. Suppose I registered me a brand like this: ⋀⋀ ."

"The Rockin' M!" O'Keefe read the final brand aloud, understanding dawning in his voice. "By God!"

"Exactly! Rework the Triangle so: ⋀⋀ . And the JM: ⋀⋀ . And the Double L: ⋀⋀ and the T Down: ⋀⋀ . The Lazy 9 doesn't work quite so well as the others, which maybe accounts for its bein' left alone at first; but it can be done, and not what you'd call a *bad* job, either. One of the points of the M is blurred a bit, but maybe the iron slipped, eh? ⋀⋀ . . . Our cattle went to Talbert's Rockin' M, Tim. It was the fired strip that fooled us, see? They knew we'd think they were headin' for the hills, so they burned over what we'd think was their trail and turned the cattle sharp into the wind and *away* from the hills, toward Talbert's! That's why the burned strip was set so far to the southwest, *sabe?* It wasn't caused by the fire backin' up; it was actually set from Talbert's!"

"So it's Jim Talbert that's doin' the rustlin'!" Tim spat disgustedly. "And him getting himself made the leader o' the vigilantes!"

"Not exactly. Read that." Ace handed the letter he had just received across to O'Keefe. O'Keefe read, and for a full minute his remarks were unprintable. Ace let him finish.

"Second the motion!" he said gravely. "So you see, Tim, how it was. Luckert, or Farley, rather, did the rustlin' and turned the beef over to Talbert to be rebranded with Talbert's Rockin' M. But Talbert would take a good-sized cut of the profits, of course, for the risk he was runnin'; so Farley got greedy and started sleeperin' Triangle calves. That way, you see, he could run his own Horseshoe on 'em later and sell 'em openly without cuttin' with Talbert. He explained the shortage of Triangle beef to Cameron by sayin' stock was bein' rustled, provin' it by the fact that other brands was also losin' stuff. Then, when the talk about rustlin' got big enough and somebody suggested organizin' vigilantes, Luckert and Talbert jumped right in and swung the thing to suit themselves. I wasn't at the meetin', but I'll bet a hat that Luckert, or one of his men—one of the men he's been importin' from the south; his old gang down there—one of them put Talbert's name up to lead the vigilantes. Smart work, you see? You can't catch a thief when the thief knows where you're goin' to look! And Talbert would put Luckert wise to every move the vigilantes made, so that Luckert could leave false trails which Talbert would see were followed."

"Oh, it's plain enough, now yuh've drawed it out in pictures for me! Yuh said at the start yuh smelled a rat in this vigilante stuff. Did yuh know all this then?"

"No. I stayed out of this vigilantes business for the very reason I gave Robertson: because I've seen it

worked that way before, and mostly it was either innocent men, or the no-'count deuces of the pack, that got
hung. I did have a hunch that there was more to all
that talk than was showin' plain on the surface; but I
didn't know any of *this!*"

"Well, it's all over now but the shoutin'! Maybe we'll
get a decent scrap out of them phoney cowboys up at
the Triangle, though. Yuh aim t' ride right in on 'em,
or sort o' surround 'em, maybe?"

"I'll lay you a little bet, Tim, that we don't find Luckert at the Triangle! I'll even take odds that we don't
find *any* of the crew there except maybe Tony, the
horse wrangler, who's been with Cameron since I was
a kid!"

"What's this, Ace? Some more o' yuhr hunches, or
are yuh bettin' a sure thing?"

"It's a hunch, mostly. I told Steve the night he came
home about the sleepers we found on his range. I figure
he must've jumped Luckert about it the next day. My
guess is that his talk with Luckert was what sent him
and Kay down here. . . . But—we'll ride in with our
guns loose, just the same! I might be wrong!"

"Yuh might be; but I ain't takin' no bets! Yuh got a
habit o' bein' right; and it seems t' be growin' on yuh!
With yuhr mind-readin' gifts, I'd be makin' me a for-
tune at poker and t' hell with cow-punchin'! It makes
corns on yuh in the wrong places, punchin' does!"

There was silence between them for a little while.
Then Tim looked up, frowning a little. "What'd yuh
mean by sayin' the guy that brought that letter is dead,
Ace?"

"That's easy! Tex Masters held him up and took him
prisoner right here in the bunkhouse, accordin' to Squint.
That's how-come he didn't have the pearl-handled gun
when he left with Masters. The mere fact that he came
here will be proof enough to Luckert that he came to
talk, won't it? And—what would be your idea of what
Wilbur's right-hand man would do to a traitor?" Ace's
voice was grim.

"Three guesses! . . . Sure. Yuh're right again . . . I

ain't got much use for double-crossers, ordinarily; but this hombre might not've been so bad, takin' him by the large. A man that's got that much gratitude in him ain't all bad, I reckon."

"Bread cast upon the waters, you know, Tim. What's the rest of it?"

"Somethin' about it comin' back to yuh all done up in chicken sandwiches, or somethin'; only that ain't the way it generally works. The bread generally gets water-logged and plumb unpleasant!"

"This piece came back, all right. I just wasn't here to —see whether it was chicken sandwiches or not. I'm sorry, too. It might've been—white meat!"

The remount came up to the tune of a lively thunder of hoofs and the white stallion broke free from Squint to greet Ace boisterously, head tossing and eyes wild in make-believe. O'Keefe had turned to the bunkhouse door as the horses appeared, calling the men out. They mounted stiffly, cursing a little as saddle-sore muscles protested against this new abuse. Ace turned in the saddle to watch them string out behind him and his throat tightened a bit with pride in them. Not a man of them but would have given his next month's pay for eight hours of sleep right now; and that eight hours would have been more than they had had in the past seventy-two. Nor was that even the least beginning in the measure of their loyalty. He knew that; knew that each would risk life, and give it, unthinkingly, in his service, if the need came. To them, it would be part of the day's work; the natural, matter-of-fact allegiance of a man to his brand.

Even now they might be riding into just that test. In his heart, he hoped that it might not turn out that way; that his guess concerning Luckert's move might prove correct. He had laughed at Cal James for saying that Luckert's riders were gunmen, but he had known even then that it was true. If Luckert and those Texas warriors were at the Triangle now there would be smoky argument before any debate with them was won. Men who had ridden with Buck Wilbur would not give up

tamely, that was sure! There were too many accounts to
be settled against them, if ever they were caught. But
Ace would prefer other battlegrounds than the ranch
yard of the Triangle, now that Kay and Ruth were there.

Buck Wilbur's right-hand man—Wes Farley. It seemed
hard to think of Wes Luckert by that name. He remembered now how Tommy Hitchcock had stopped Luckert's draw that night in the Palace Bar, and how he had
cursed Luckert for a fool for daring to make gun-play
against Gilbert. "Don't do that, Luckert, yuh damn fool!"
Tommy had said. "Yuh want t' get killed?" It had never
occurred to Tommy that any man in Utah might stand
a chance against the speed of Ace Gilbert's hands! He
wondered if Tommy would have been as sure had he
known that Luckert was Farley. gun-throwing aide to a
leader of bad men, cold-blooded killer by trade? But
they had fought with fists instead of guns, and in that
battle, Gilbert had won. Wes Farley would never forgive
that defeat, either. Thunder River range would not be
safe for Gilbert while Farley or his men rode within its
boundaries.

"Not that that makes any difference," Ace told himself. "I've been in this war ever since the first shot hit
Eddy Lane out there by the ford! It's him or me, now;
no quarter and no holds barred!"

Behind him as they rode Ace could hear Tim O'Keefe
passing on the news of Ace's letter to the men. Just now
O'Keefe was venturing a doubt as to his boss's infallibil-
ity: "Ace figgers they'll be gone when we get there, but
keepin' my fingers crossed means anything he's goin' to
be wrong! Just one shot at the skunks that downed Eddy
—that's all I ask! I ain't smelled smoke since Hector was
a mere pup, but my trigger finger is sure itchin' now!"

Someone back there growled an answer that was in
full keeping with Gilbert's thoughts of a moment past:
"Yuh ain't braggin', are yuh, Tim? Or do yuh figger
yuh'll be in this fight alone?"

They halted on a bit of higher ground a little distance
from the Triangle buildings and looked long at the scene
before them while their horses champed on their bits

and stamped. The place was as peaceful as a painted landscape; empty with an emptiness that seemed ageless and unbreakable. No one spoke, but Ace loosened the reins a little and Satan stepped forward, leading the advance proudly as though he moved to martial music. Ace glanced back once and his glance swept the men behind him swiftly; came back to the front again, satisfied. The line behind him was spread out a little, leaving space between the men. And each rider was sitting loosely in his saddle at ease, with a detachment that was the acme of alertness.

But nothing stirred among the Triangle buildings or in the yard as they entered it at a running walk. And so Ace dismounted and dropped the stallion's reins and walked deliberately up the bordered path to the house. Back of him, a dozen men remained mounted, still scattered a little as if by chance; and, also by chance, perhaps, they were so placed that no part of the place remained unwatched. Good men, these cowboys! Good, loyal, men.

The door burst open as Ace set foot to the steps leading up to the porch and he halted there, learning from his own quick tension how taut his nerves had been. It was Kay who came through that door, however; Kay, with both hands outstretched to him and a welcome in her eyes that not even her incoherent words could match. He caught her hands in both of his and held them tight.

"What's wrong, Kay? . . . Where's Luckert, and the boys? . . . Where's Steve?"

"Ace! Oh, Ace, I thought you'd never come!"

He saw then that she was very near to tears, and the fact dismayed him. Kay, who never wept—who had taken her little-girl bumps and disappointments with stoic calm or man-like anger—Kay about to cry was a startling thing to Ace and he took her in his arms instinctively, shielding her face against him. Tim O'Keefe had come to stand beside them now, and Ace spoke again the question he had asked at first: "Where's Luckert, Kay?"

"He's gone! He and the boys. . . . There's nobody left but Tony!"

Ace glanced aside at Tim, his lips twitching ever so slightly in the ghost of a smile. O'Keefe made a face at him.

"What's happened, Kay? Shucks, imp! You're not cryin', are you? Tell me what's gone wrong?"

"Of course—I'm not!" She sniffed a bit, suspiciously; but she pulled away from him and showed him a face under control again. And then she told in swift, clean sentences all that had happened since the night when she had seen him last.

"Wes meant what he said about—not hurting dad," she said, at the end. "And I was afraid if I went to Sheriff Robertson that what I said might do more harm than good. Luckert *said* it would ruin dad, you know; the—truth, I mean. And the other man thought so, too. So—I told Gordon all about it, and he agreed with me. He thought, as I did, that it would be best to wait until we could talk to you. . . . But it's been—hard to wait, Ace. Thinking of dad, a prisoner—fearing that I hadn't done the right thing, after all. . . . But, don't you see, I *couldn't* risk the other thing, either? Politics—his position in the state—all means so much to him. . . ."

"I reckon you did the only thing, Kay. . . . So Wallace stood pat, eh? I'd have bet on him to do that! And Ruth? She's worried. too, of course . . ."

"We—didn't tell Ruth, Ace. Gordon thought we might as well save her the worry of it, if we could. We told her dad was called away on business; be back after the —fifteenth. She and Gordon rode in to the Wells this morning. There's a dance being planned. . . ." She laughed a little; a dance at such a time seemed oddly out of place, somehow! "It's for Saturday night—the sixteenth. Gordon's leaving Sunday. It's in his honor, you see."

"This other man, Kay; the one they were waiting for up there on the bluff: Did you see him?"

"Yes. He was a stranger to me; a man with a black beard, cut spade-fashion under his chin."

Ace chuckled and Tim O'Keefe swore softly and apologized. Kay looked at Ace inquiringly and he explained. "That's Talbert, imp; owns the Rockin' M. He's new, since you left. Tim's sore because I've happened to guess right about a thing or two, today! You see, Tim, it isn't 'all over but the shoutin',' after all! First we've got to catch Farley!"

Kay's quick question gave Ace his turn to tell his own discoveries, and minutes passed while they fitted together the various bits of knowledge in their hands.

"Well, anyway," O'Keefe said, finally, "it won't be much of a trick t' catch 'em! Not since we know that they're plannin' to stick up the bank, and when! All we got t' do . . ."

A man called suddenly from the yard, cutting O'Keefe's suggestion short. "There's a lot o' men ridin' this way from the east, Ace. Headin' here, looks like. What d'yuh want t' do?"

Ace stood up quickly, staring hard at the approaching cavalcade. It was a moment before he spoke; a moment in which the horsemen yonder came into clearer view. "It's Robertson," he said, at last. "Looks like a posse!" And then, later: "The man on the bay, at Robertson's left—That's the man you saw up on the bluff, isn't it, Kay?"

"Why—yes! Yes, it is! What's he doing? . . ."

"Let me do the talkin', now!" Ace's voice was curt, abstracted. The men with Robertson were deploying now as Ace's men had deployed a while ago. Robertson had seen the horsemen in the yard and was approaching warily. But he must have recognized the men, finally; for he made a quick gesture with his hand and spurred in toward them, followed by his men. Ace stepped down from the porch. "Howdy, Dave," he said. "What's up?"

"Bank's been robbed," Robertson said shortly. "Wes Luckert and a couple o' Triangle punchers pulled the job; walked into the bank and told White they wanted t' arrange a loan. Luckert claimed he aimed t' start a spread of his own. White took 'em back t' his office, and they knocked him out. Used the office as a vantage point from which they had the drop on the whole shebang! Nobody even knew anything was happenin' until they were ridin' out and the cashier yelled. . . . We come straight here. Seen yuhr men in the yard and thought maybe we was in luck! . . . Is Luckert here?"

"Foolish question, Dave," Ace told him, gently. "And —his name isn't Luckert! It's—Wes Farley!"

The sheriff stared at Ace for a moment.

"Wes Farley! You don't mean—"

"Yes," said Ace grimly, "That's who I mean—One-shot Farley, Wilbur's right-hand man!"

## 10 • "YOU WIN, GILBERT"

THERE WAS a moment of astonished silence, followed by a volley of incredulous talk. From the corner of his eye, Ace had watched Jim Talbert's face as he made his charge, curious to note its effect. But Talbert's expression showed nothing more than the shocked surprise that appeared on Robertson's face, and all the rest. The man was a good actor! But then, he had been prepared! Ace remembered now that Red Curtis had gone from the Lazy 9 bunkhouse in the custody of Masters. Talbert would guess, then, that Ace knew. And that realization explained other things, as well! It explained why this robbery had been moved ahead two days, for one thing! Knowing that Curtis had betrayed him, Farley had simply set his schedule ahead to forestall any further spreading of the facts. It was simple, once one had the key!

Dave Robertson blustered a little. "Don't be a fool, Ace! Yuh never liked Wes, and I reckon this justifies yuh some. No doubt about him pullin' this job, sure.

But there's no use stickin' a charge like that on him besides! I've got a dozen descriptions o' Farley, at the office; and they don't tally with Luckert, a-tall! Height and weight, yes; but Farley was a blond! Luckert's hair is black!"

"Either Wes Farley was bleached, or Wes Luckert is dyed, then." Ace refused to be shaken. If Red Curtis would risk his life for gratitude he would not risk it for a lie! "I reckon you and me are due for a little talk, Dave—alone! Mind steppin' inside the house a minute?"

He stepped back toward the door, and Robertson swung down from his saddle, muttering. Jim Talbert dismounted, too, and came forward in the Sheriff's wake. Ace frowned a little. "Alone is what I said, Dave," he said pointedly. Talbert halted scowling.

"I ain't meanin' to butt in, Gilbert," he said. "But, as leader o' the vigilantes, I thought . . ."

"This is bein' handled by the law, Talbert; not the vigilantes." Ace's smile was unfathomable as he gave way for Robertson to pass and then stepped through the door, closing it behind him.

Robertson faced him inside the room, hands on hips. "Well, Ace? What's all the hocus-pocus mean?"

"I reported the murder of one of my men the other day, Dave. You found the killer yet?"

"Yuh know I ain't, Ace! Case like that, there ain't one chance in ten of ever findin' 'em! Yuh know that! I rode out there; got a lot o' measurements of the tracks, and some empty shells. I follered the trail to where they burned it out; seen where yuh went on to the hills. Yuh're as good a trailer as there is in the country, Ace. *Yuh* didn't find anything, did yuh?"

"Not by trailin', no! . . . And now, this bank job. What's Talbert's rank in your posse, Dave? Sort of a general adviser?"

"No more'n anybody else, I reckon. He was on the spot and I deputized him. Luckert's trail came into the main traveled road and we came here first, thinkin' he might've come this way."

"Talbert suggest comin' here?"

"No! . . . Yes, maybe he did. Hell! I don't know! We all thought it was as good an idea as any! What yuh drivin' at, anyway?"

"Wes Luckert is Wes Farley, Dave. I *know* that! And Jim Talbert is his right-hand man! I know *that,* too! You won't find Luckert as long as you follow Talbert's tips; and if you do find him, and Talbert is with you, you'll have a traitor beside you! Talbert'll be fightin' for Luckert, not for you!"

Dave Robertson stared for a moment incredulously. Then his head went back, and he laughed. "Yuh don't expect me t' believe that, do yuh, Ace? Why, Talbert was the first one t' start the fireworks in town today! Luckert and his pals was ridin' out, hell-fer-leather, firin' back so that the street was fair choked with hot lead! And Talbert jumped right out behind 'em and started emptyin' his sixes! Yuh're all right, Ace; but yuh got a grudge against Luckert and yuh're on the prod over this vigilante business, so yuh just can't see straight about anything connected with either of 'em! I ain't blamin' yuh; been that way myself! But . . ."

"Talbert didn't drop anybody, with all his shootin', did he?" Ace's voice was grim now; angry.

"No! What o' that? I was shootin', too, and I didn't hit! Plenty o' lead goes wild when men are surprised that way!"

"And Talbert wasn't hit, either, was he? Luckert wasn't surprised, you know! He was expectin' a fight! But I notice Talbert's wearin' a new, white hat! Right easy to recognize, that hat! . . . And, of course, Talbert's jumpin' out in the middle of the street didn't hinder anybody's else's shootin', did it?"

Robertson raised his hand, angry now in turn. "That's enough, Ace! I ain't goin' t' hold this against yuh, but —I ain't listenin' t' no more talk like that, *sabe?* If yuh got anything t' say that's reasonable, I'll listen. Otherwise, I'm goin'! I'm human, and I make mistakes; but I ain't bein' carried away by my own prejudices like yuh are!"

"Prejudices! I can prove it, Dave, you blasted fool! I

. . ." But the unbelieving light in Robertson's eyes stopped him. "All right, Dave! Go ahead! I told you once that Lazy 9 would fight its own battles, remember? Well, that goes! There were some things I aimed to tell you, but I won't now! You go ahead and find 'em out for yourself! You quit mighty easy when it came to findin' Eddy Lane's killers! Left it up to me! All right, let it go that way!"

It was foolish, and Gilbert knew it even as he spoke. But he was too angry now to care!

"Yuh hintin' that I'm neglectin' my duty about that killin', Ace?" Robertson's voice was hard now. "That's fightin' talk, son! Man ought to be ready t' back his play when he talks like that!"

"You know me, Dave. I've never made a play yet I wouldn't back! But I'm not fightin' you, you stubborn fool! Go on and play it your own way! I'll do the same!"

Robertson hesitated a moment; turned angrily to the door. "Stubborn, eh?" he growled. "Seems t' me yuh're stubborn as a mare-mule, yuhrself, by God! . . . All right, though." He jerked the door open and stalked outside. "Come on, boys. Nothin' here for us! So long, Ace! See yuh when yuh're in yuhr right mind again!"

Tim O'Keefe followed Robertson with his eyes, then turned to Ace and made a sucking sound with his tongue. "Yuh wouldn't say he was mad, or anything, would yuh?" he asked. "What'd yuh say t' him t' make him go off in a huff that way, Ace?"

"I told him the truth—or part of it; and he laughed at me! Made me mad, and I acted like a fool! Told him to go on and play it his own way, then, and I'd play my own hand the same way!"

"I wouldn't call that actin' the fool, exactly," Tim said judiciously. "I'd just call it selfish! Keepin' all the fightin', and the glory, and the fun, in the fam'ly, so to speak! I'm in favor of it! Besides, I was beginnin' t' figger yuh was infallible, or somethin'. Glad t' find out yuh can get mad and make mistakes and act human, like the rest of us!" He grinned impudently and swaggered out to impart the tidings to the rest of the crew. That his own views were shared unanimously there was proved by the exultant shout that went up, and Ace smiled a little in spite of himself.

"You didn't tell him—about Dad, did you, Ace?" Kay's voice broke ever so little and Ace turned to her and laid his arm over her shoulder protectingly.

"Of course, Kay darlin'! Mind my callin' yuh that, imp? You *are,* you know! Darlin' imp!" He tipped her face up a little, laughing down into her eyes. "And don't you worry your head about that dad of yours!" he told her. "Steve Cameron never did a really bad thing in his life, and don't you believe he did! He'll be comin' back soon now, I reckon, since Luckert's cat is out of the bag already."

"I don't really think Dad could have done anything— bad, Ace. But—it's been sort of hard to keep—smiling— when I couldn't keep from worrying about him—and *you,* you big bum!"

"That's right! Call me names! That's gratitude, now, for all the lolly-pops I've brought you! . . . Seriously, Kay, you mustn't worry about me, you know. The slug with my name on it hasn't been cast yet! And Mr. Wes Luckert, alias Wes Farley, or vice versa, is goin' to be too busy dodgin' trouble to go lookin' for any more!"

"I'll take up that lolly-pop remark with you some other time, Lord Gil! And in the meantime, what are you going to do?" Her voice had its old, impudent ring now and Ace patted her shoulder approvingly.

"Why, right now I'm goin' to send my boys down to your bunkhouse and let them catch about eight hours sleep! Then I'm goin' to send you off somewhere while I set my so-called brain to work figuring out a cagey plot . . . And after that . . ."

"Ace! There's Dad! See? Just coming down the hill yonder, to the north! That's his disreputable old hat— and I'd recognize White Stockings as far as I could see!"

"It's him, all right! . . . Now, what'd I tell you? Run in and powder your nose, now, while I send the boys to bed! He'll be ten minutes gettin' here. . . ."

She whirled obediently and ran indoors. Ace chuckled a little as he walked down into the yard. Sweet kid, Kay! None better! Game, and smart as a whip! "If I wasn't in love with Ruth," he thought, "I'd fall for Kay as sure as! . . ." He halted suddenly and turned, staring back at the door through which she had gone. "I'll be damned!" He chuckled softly. "I reckon you're right about bein' grown up, imp! Must be! Or I wouldn't be thinkin' thoughts like that. . . ."

"Yuh want me, Ace?"

Tim O'Keefe spoke at Gilbert's back and Ace turned, startled and a little chagrined. "Was I talkin' out loud, Tim?" he asked.

"Yeah. What thoughts was them yuh was mentionin', anyway?"

"Go to hell, Tim! . . . You and the boys go down to the bunkhouse and turn in. Or—I reckon the cook is still on the job, if you want chow first. But don't miss the sleep, *sabe?* We'll be ridin' tonight again; so get some rest."

"Hell, we don't need rest, Ace! Say the word, and we'll get goin'! No use wastin' time . . ."

"It isn't bein' wasted, Tim. Luckert is holed up somewhere by now, and he won't be movin' much in daylight for a while. Tonight is time enough."

"O.K. . . . Better watch yuhrself, Ace! Now that Miss Kay's grown up, as yuh was sayin' a minute ago, she's plumb dangerous for an engaged man like yuh!"

Tim escaped Gilbert's grasp by an inch and ran; and Ace stood, laughing a little, awaiting Steve Cameron's arrival. Kay joined him in a moment, but not for long. Cameron had still a quarter of a mile to go when Kay's patience ran out and she sped to meet him. So they came back together, Steve Cameron and his girl; Kay perched precariously on his saddle bow inside the circle of his arms.

Steve Cameron made no attempt to avoid the issue. "I owe yuh an apology, Ace," he said. "Yuh was right about Wes. I knew yuh was, at the time; but—I tried givin' him another chance. Yuh see . . . Wes is my kid brother, Ace. That's why I was—protectin' him!"

The statement struck Gilbert like a blow in the face. His jaw dropped and he stood staring for a moment, slow to believe the evidence of his ears. When he closed his mouth at last he was grinning; a grin with little humor in it. "O'Keefe should have been here," he said slowly. "I've been makin' some lucky guesses today. Tim would have enjoyed seein' me take a surprise square on the chin! . . . I reckon we've got a lot of talkin' to do, Steve; the three of us."

They walked together to the porch and sat down there. For a long moment, no one spoke. Ace shrugged at last and broke the silence. Tersely, without embellishment, he told the story of the past three days since he had left the Triangle on the night of Eddy Lane's death. Steve Cameron listened, and once, when Ace had told of Red Curtis's visit to the Lazy 9, he interrupted.

"He paid for that note, Ace; with his life! I saw him —murdered!"

Ace nodded. "I figured that," he said. "He told me in that note that Wes Luckert was—Wes Farley, Steve. That cleared things up, for me."

"So! So yuh know that! . . . Well, go on."

"After we combed the Mescaleros for sign and failed to find even a trace, I got to thinkin' about that burned strip that had blotted out the trail. I told you it ran northeast clear to the hills, and southwest to Talbert's place, as near as we could tell. So I got to thinkin' about Talbert's Rockin' M brand. I got it pretty clear in my mind, and then I got home to find Curtis's note. That cinched it." He sketched rapidly the manner in which the Rocking M could be used to blot the various brands on the Thunder River range. "So that's the end of it; my part of it, that is. Kay's got a yarn to tell, too, before we listen to yours."

"So it's Talbert! . . . That's news to me, sure! All right, Kay?"

Kay's story was quickly told, and when it was done: "We didn't tell Ruth, Dad. You see, what Luckert said about—about it hurting you if the truth were told—that frightened me, you understand? I was afraid that—telling —might hurt you worse than being prisoner could!"

Steve Cameron's arm tightened about his daughter's shoulder. "Poor kid," he said. "I've told you, now, why —what Wes meant by that. You see, we were orphaned, Wes and I, when he was only ten. I took care of him. He was a wild kid; got so he hated the discipline I tried to enforce. Maybe I was too harsh. . . . The responsibility of bein' dad and mother to him weighed pretty heavily on me; yuh can see how that might be. I was only eighteen when we were left alone. . . . So Wes ran away. I never heard from him once in more than twenty years, and then—he came here. He was fifteen when he left me. Those years had made—a different man of him. He told me he was the man known in the south as Wes Farley, that he'd been hand in glove with Buck Wilbur; that he was—wanted. He said he wanted to reform; start over. He told me he'd been smart enough down there to disguise himself; bleach his hair, and wear a mustache, and change his name. He swore he'd go straight if I'd give him a chance. . . . Yuh see how it was with me, Ace? He was my own blood! . . . I let him persuade me. Gave him a job. He's a good cattleman. I thought he was makin' good, and I gave him every chance; made him range boss; trusted him. . . . When yuh told me what yuh did the other night, I knew in my heart it was true, but—it was like a knife stickin' into me! I refused to admit that I believed it. I put it up to Wes the next mornin' and he laughed at me! Said he'd just used me all along as a shield, waitin' till he could get his old cronies here to start the Arizona stuff all over again. And he taunted me with the fact that I was guilty with him; accessory after the fact, you see? I'd sheltered and kept a criminal, knowingly. . . . That's what he meant, up there on the bluff, Kay. And he was right. This ends my political life, all right. But that won't keep me from doin' my duty and tellin' the truth!"

There was a pause while Steve Cameron measured in

his mind the cost of this thing he was about to do. "I went straight to the Lazy 9 to tell yuh the truth, Ace. Yuh was gone. I followed yuh, and was caught. Yuh know all that. This mornin', a man brought a prisoner t' Wes; this man, Curtis. Wes was holdin' me, yuh know, t' keep the fact of his identity a secret until after this bank robbery was over. Then he found out that the news was out; that Curtis had left a note for yuh. Curtis told him about the note; taunted him; laughed at him. He was a brave man, Ace, this Red Curtis, no matter what he tried t' do t' yuh once. . . . Wes shot him! Deliberately shot down an unarmed man! . . . It was horrible! Ace, the man is a beast! A mad, blood-crazed animal! Brother or not, I'd shoot him down with my own hand to rid the world of him! It—sickened me! . . . Well, they figured they could hit town and rob the bank before yuh could spread the news. I thought Wes was goin' to kill me then, knowin' I'd seen what he did to Curtis. But he didn't seem to care! They turned me loose, leadin' my horse with 'em a few miles so I'd have to walk long enough to delay me so's I couldn't do anything to block 'em. And—here I am."

It was Ace who broke the silence following. "You won't have to do any killin', Steve," he said. "I aim to tend to that—myself! . . . And, about this other thing: his bein' your brother, I mean. Let's keep that just between ourselves for a while, eh? Wallace ought to know, since he knows the rest of it. But—no one else, *sabe?*"

Cameron shrugged. "I don't see what good it'll do, Ace. But—whatever yuh say."

"Good! . . . Ruth and Wallace are comin now, so remember: You've been to Junction City, on business!"

Ruth Cameron and her guest made a boisterous entrance later, both agog with news of the bank robbery in town. "By George!" Wallace exclaimed, beaming. "It was great! My special benefit, you might say! Welcome home, Colonel Cameron! I hope your—ah—trip wasn't too strenuous, eh?"

"Thanks, Wallace. No, not strenuous; but—I'm glad to be home!"

Wallace grinned amiably and winked past Ruth's shoulder at Ace. But there was no trace of any undercurrent of meaning in the talk that sped on merrily. Wallace described the hold-up as he had seen it with a verve and enthusiasm that set them all to laughing. "It was splendid!" he insisted. "Your Wild West is better than the moving pictures, even! And imagine me being right on the spot, eh? *Splendid!* Wouldn't have missed it for the world!"

"He didn't miss a thing, either, believe me!" Ruth told them. "He was like a small boy at a circus parade; right out in the street—bullets flying all around him—eyes big as dollars, with his mouth wide open! Laughing! Yes, sir! Picture of a kid having the time of his life!"

"I was, too! Couldn't help laughing, 'pon my word! Chap near me was jumping around and firing off a gun—so help me, he was shooting faster than I could count; making a racket fit to wake the dead! Funny thing was, he was shooting straight up in the air! Must have thought the blasted robbers had wings! He jumped around so his hat fell off! I handed it to him afterward, and he looked it over carefully for holes! Swore it'd been shot off his head!"

Ace chuckled in sympathy with the man's unfeigned delight. "White hat, wasn't it?" he asked, later. "Man with a spade beard?"

"Oh, I say, Gilbert! How did you know?"

"Thought it must have been. Man by the name of Talbert, that was."

Kay shot a quick glance at Ace. "Still using the old powers of deduction, eh, Lord Gil? I'll tell Tim on you!"

The group divided soon, leaving Ace and Gordon Wallace alone. There was a blank silence for a time, and Ace broke it awkwardly. "Kay says you're leavin' us soon, Wallace. I'm sorry. I'm afraid we haven't entertained you very well; at least, I haven't. Things have piled up . . ."

"I know. No apologies, Gilbert. Understand perfectly. Never had a better time in my life, anyway! Like to

have seen more of you, and all that. . . . Yes, I'm running along. Word today—business in California all ready
to sign on dotted line. Nuisance, and all that sort of
thing. Still, may be a good thing, too. Matter of an es-
tate being settled, you see? Gives me a chance to handle the principal instead of just a monthly dole. Like to
talk to you sometime about investing something out here;
land; cattle; that sort of thing." It was a long speech
for Wallace. Ace waited, wondering a little.

"Don't mean here, exactly." Wallace dropped his eyes
and shrugged slightly. "Wouldn't want to be a blasted
nuisance; rejected swain—that sort of thing. You win,
you know, Gilbert. Told you you would, remember? Best
man wins, and so on? Damned cheeky of me to put
in my oar! Sporting of you to—let me! Shake hands,
will you?"

They shook hands, both painfully conscious that the
gesture was overdone. The silence settled upon them
again, dismally. Later, Ace related the facts of Steve
Cameron's return and of his relationship with his captor.
Wallace nodded; made dry comment. "Wes Luckert—Wes
Farley—I suppose it's Wes Cameron, really, eh? Chap's
as elusive as the devil, eh? Put a name on him and it
slips off! Unpleasant devil whatever you call him!"

And so the talk drifted stiltedly to other things. But
Ace's thoughts were strangely muddled; abstracted; un-
sure. Ordinarily he had straight, clear-cut opinions of
people and things; thought processes that moved in an
orderly fashion from fact to fact. But not now. He was
vaguely pleased with the knowledge that Ruth Cameron
had been loyal to him, and yet—he knew an honest regret that her loyalty had hurt this other man. He liked
Wallace; would be sorry to see him go. It even occurred
to him to wonder *why* Ruth had chosen the way she
had done. Wallace had a polish—a culture—a poise that
Ace Gilbert would never attain. Those things, in the
degree that Wallace had them, came from a world with
which Ace was unfamiliar; from a background of travel
and contacts with people in whom the social, gentle

graces were inbred. And those were the things that Ruth Cameron admired. Those were the things that seemed to fit her.

It puzzled him.

# 11 · DRAGNET

IT WAS dark when Ace Gilbert awoke after seven hours of refreshing sleep, and he sat up at once, pulling on his boots while he sniffed at the odors of coffee and food that came to him faintly from the back of the house. Kay Cameron met him in the main room.

"Feel better?" she asked.

"Great! I smell supper cookin'; which, to my infallible mind, proves that you've had a session with the cook and are prepared to offer hospitality. Thanks, Kay. I was so dead for sleep I forgot that."

"Did you think I'd let you go away hungry? Cookie is putting up packages of sandwiches, too. I heard you say you'd be riding tonight, you know. . . . And there are men outside using horrible language because I wouldn't let them wake you! Better go and soothe their ruffled tempers!"

"Who?"

"Cal James and four cowboys; Tommy Hitchcock and five of the same; Tubby Martin and eight." She enumerated them swiftly on her fingers. "That makes twenty, if my addition is up to par. Can you handle them all, or shall I send for the cavalry?"

"I can handle 'em, I reckon. . . . What the devil do they want, anyway?"

"Ask them! I'm too busy to bother with the wants of a lot of men! And supper will be ready in ten minutes."

He grinned as she slipped past him toward the kitchen; walked quickly to the porch and into the clutches of three impatient men. Their voices made a bedlam for a moment, until Cal James gained supremacy of spokesmanship.

". . . And here we are! What the hell, Ace? Tryin' to hog it yourself?" James was indignant.

"You're here, all right! I can see that! But why? Say it one at a time, and slow, please! What is it I'm tryin' to hog?"

"This Luckert business! I heard about the bank robbery and got to town too late to join the posse. Chased 'em here, and Cameron told me about Eddy Lane and that yuh was aimin' to do things. Yuh was asleep, so I sent Cameron's wrangler up to the JM for Tubby and rode down to Tommy's myself. Tubby sent a man for my boys, and we're all here and loaded for bear! What's the order?"

Ace grinned a little. "First thing is, find your bear!" he said. "Who told you boys I wanted help? Why didn't you toddle along to Talbert and get him to gather his vigilantes?"

"Listen, Ace." It was Hitchcock speaking now, very seriously. "We went to that meetin' when the vigilantes was organized, and when we found out yuh wasn't there the three of us got together and had a talk. We doped it out this way: Dave Robertson is a good man, but he's no great shakes as a sheriff. Talbert may be a good man or not; he's a newcomer and we don't know him. We *do* know *you!* So we decided what was good enough for the Lazy 9 was good enough for us! Cal and me, we're just deuce-low compared t' the big spreads like yuhr's, anyway. Tubby's outfit is maybe about a ten-spot, but he's with us in this. Yuh're the Ace! We aim t' trail along with yuh, whether yuh like it or not; and this thing shapes up like a real serious proposition. Luckert seems to be throwin' in with the wild bunch, and he's took a dozen or more men with him. This Eddy Lane killin' means that the rustlers have widened their loop t' take in the Lazy 9; which means none of us are safe. When I heard that, I knew yuh'd be ridin' and I knew yuh'd keep ridin' till the job was done. Yuh're the man we aim t' follow! So—what's the orders?"

Ace nodded slowly. "I said I'd go it alone," he protested again.

"Yuh got no choice, yuh stubborn fool! We're here! Yuh try givin' us the slip now and we'll stretch yuhr hide on a barb' wire frame!"

Gilbert grinned suddenly. "All right!" he said. "Orders, you want, eh? Here's one: Cal, dash down and get O'Keefe and my boys out o' their bunks! Get 'em washed up and herded into the mess-hall, pronto! I'll talk then. Rest of you, do the same with your boys. Ten minutes, Kay said; and the man that's late gets the job of holdin' the horses if we hit a fight!"

And so it was over a final cup of steaming coffee that the plan was laid. Ace Gilbert pushed his chair back a bit and outlined his campaign. "There's thirty-two of us, not countin' myself," he said. "I want you split up into sixteen pairs. Each pair leaves here separately and rides to one of the places I'll name. Cookie has packages of grub for you; but go light on it, because there's no tellin' how long we'll be out or how soon I can get more food to you. I've picked out spots from which the lot of us should be able to see about every move that's made on this range. Get to 'em without bein' seen, and once you're there, lay low. I'll ride the rounds myself, and take any reports anybody has to make. You all know who we're lookin' for: Luckert! If anybody see's Luckert's outfit he's to trail 'em and send his party on to notify the nearest pair to his location. Then one of the second party goes on to notify the next pair while the other two follow the first man. And so on. Choose your partners and I'll give you your locations."

They chose quickly and Ace named for each pair a vantage spot. "It makes a big circle," he said, when he had done. "Remember, Luckert's outfit will be watchin' the range too; so when I say lay low, I mean just that! No fires; no movin' about. When I ride past you, talk fast because I won't stop! Say somethin', whether you've seen anything or not, though; because if nobody speaks I'll know you've started closin' in. In that case, I'll expect to find a note in your hidin' place tellin' me which way to ride. Don't forget that, now! And—nobody's to bust into a fight until I've joined you, *sabe?* . . . Everybody got it? Then get goin'!"

They filed out swiftly, but Tim O'Keefe paused in the doorway. "What hoss yuh aimin' t' ride, Ace?" he asked.

"Why, Satan, I reckon."

"Not by a damn sight, yuh don't! That hoss is a walkin' request for trouble, times like these! Yuh get one o' Cameron's broncs, see? I'll saddle one for yuh. . . . And for Pete's sake, Ace, use some judgment yuhrself, will yuh? Luckert's lookin' for yuh, special; and yuh're askin' for murder anyway, ridin' the range alone like yuh're plannin'!"

"We're all takin' a chance, Tim. . . . But I'll not ride Satan, if it worries you. Ask Steve if I can take his big sorrel?"

And so the dragnet was set. Out across the length and breadth of the Thunder River range, pairs of horsemen rode warily through the night to lookout posts from which they could keep a sharp vigilance upon the entire valley; posts spaced widely by necessity, but so chosen that the cordon was complete.

Later, on the big white-stockinged sorrel that was Steve Cameron's favorite mount, Ace Gilbert began the rounds that were to be his for the next three days and nights. He rode west first; west from the Triangle toward Jim Talbert's Rocking M. A trail ran that way, but Ace avoided it; rode parallel to the beaten way until he reached the point where the trail ran between two twisted trees at the top of a long divide. He slowed his pace as he neared those trees, and by way of camouflage for his leisurely gait, began to roll a cigarette. There was bright moonlight on that hilltop, but the trees cast deep shadow about the cluster rocks at their base and Ace saw no living thing. A voice came to him as he passed, however; a voice that he recognized as Martin's:

"Not a creature was stirrin', not even a mouse!" the voice said. "And bring me a cushion next time yuh come around! These rocks are hard!"

He swung southward then, toward the ford where Eddy Lane had met his death. Other voices spoke to him from time to time, each one from an unseen source. At the old branding corral Tim O'Keefe greeted Ace with oaths: "Keep t' the valleys, yuh damn fool!" he said. "I've watched yuh against the sky for a mile! What d'yuh think we're runnin'? A shootin' gallery?"

And so it went on and on, interminably. Mid-afternoon of the fourteenth brought one bit of news from Cal James. "Robertson's see-sawin' back and forth like a hound dog in coon country!" he said. "Talbert's gone home and got out all his boys and Dave deputized 'em as a second posse with Talbert in charge! Dave's dumb as hell!"

But there was no word of Luckert still. Robertson's possemen were scouting the Mescalero foothills. Talbert's riders were striking westward, along the river. Robertson was out of the hills now and riding south. Talbert had turned back and was going over the ground Robertson had just left. A nester up northeast was sick and the doctor had ridden out from the Wells, and back again. The nester would get well. One of Lyle Long's punchers was sleeping in his saddle up along Snake Creek and a tumbleweed gave his bronc an excuse to pitch. The puncher landed on the back of his neck. He would wonder throughout his life how that incident became known! And so on.

That night, Ace carride saddlebags stuffed with packets of food. He even took out a checkerboard to Martin and his partner. They would use pebbles for men; "though it's damn hard t' crown a king with 'em! There ought t' be more flat pebbles in this country! . . . Reckon Talbert must've given up, eh? I smelled coffee boilin' over that way this evenin'."

But Cal James, down by the old corral had other news. "Talbert's outfit is camped down for the night over beyond that ridge. Better swing wide and keep down wind from 'em. A horse might nicker and give yuh away."

It was a bit disturbing, that news. Coffee odors on the wind up by the Rocking M; Talbert and his riders camped south of the river. Of course, there might be other Rocking M men left at the ranch; but Cal had said yesterday that Talbert had had all of his boys deputized.

Ace stopped under the lee of a hill two miles past Cal James' hiding place and sat for a long time, thinking. It was foolish, of course; Robertson's posse had fed at the Rocking M yesterday, spending an hour or more there. Whoever was cooking coffee there tonight had a right to be there, no doubt. And possibly the coffee was only a figment of Tubby's imagination. Tubby had been for forty-eight hours already without coffee. His senses might be tantalizing him!

But—Ace turned the sorrel north in spite of all those things; sent him back toward the Rocking M at a swinging lope. The change of course brought a queer sense of prescience to Gilbert; the feeling of some inner fore-knowledge of things to come. It was as if the night range were alive with subtle messages to which he was sensitive without actual knowledge of them. He rode with a subconscious tension which he could not explain; an instinct to listen for sounds that were not audible—for movements that were not seen. The small breezes whispering down the valleys in which he rode seemed vibrant with news of other riders in other valleys, of impending events. And yet it was all intangible, unreal. He tried to shrug the feeling off, but it returned to him unwilled. Once, he stopped the sorrel and got down to lay his ear against the ground to listen for other hoofbeats. He heard nothing, and when he remounted it was with that sense of embarrassment that comes to a child who has been frightened of the dark.

A mile from the Rocking M it seemed to him that the soft thud of the sorrel's hoofs was actually mingled with fainter hoofbeats far away, and he stopped again. There was nothing; and he would not dismount this time to test the earth-vibrations with his ear. He rode on instead,

warily, along a shadowed arroyo that slanted past the
Rocking M corrals and he did not pause again until he
had come as near the house as he dared to ride. He left
the sorrel there, tied carefully to a scrubby bush. Satan
he would have trusted to stand untied, but this rangy
sorrel might have unknown ways. He might have urgent
need of the horse suddenly tonight and his vague fore-
bodings added a little to his caution.

The Rocking M ranch house was dark on the side from
which he approached it, but now, certainly, there was no
unreality in the evidence that came to him by another
sense: the sense of smell! The pungent, spicy odor of
boiling coffee was plain in the breeze drifting down
from the house and the smell of it turned Gilbert's approach into a careful stalk as a hunter might creep up
wind toward a wary game. Boiling coffee meant men in
the darkened house, and men there now might mean
danger. Ace took advantage of every shadowy cover with
the skill of an Indian; moved lightly, swiftly, silently as
a cat, to the shelter of the house itself.

There at last was comparative safety in the deeper
shade along the walls, and he slid swiftly around the
building to its other side. A horse stood with dangling
reins a little distance from a door at the rear and Ace
could see the bellows movement of his sides in the
moonlight to tell of recent labor. The beast's head was
low and he flicked one ear disinterestedly at the man
by the wall; no more. There *had* been other hoofbeats
than the sorrel's then, on the wind a while ago! This
horse had just finished a hard run; could not have been
standing here more than a minute or two—not time
enough, at least, for him to catch his breath.

Floorboards inside the house creaked a little and there
was the scrape of a chair drawn across the floor. A window just beyond the door showed a narrow crack of
light, and as Ace passed the doorstep he saw another
gleam of yellow along the sill. He halted by the window
and pressed his ear close against the curtained glass. A
man was pacing up and down the floor inside, the quick,
sharp sound of his boots seeming somehow to reflect im-

patience and smouldering anger. A door squeaked then, and thudded shut. Other footsteps sounded, drowned almost at once by the low murmur of an angry voice.

"Damn it, he had no business riskin' everything the way he's doin'! The whole range is spooky—full o' men—on edge, ready for trouble! He might've waited at least until he'd talked it over with me! He knew I was comin' tonight. Hell! It's me that's takin' the risk, ridin' everywhere with men who'd cut me down like a dog if they even guessed. . . ."

The speaker passed very near the curtained window then and Ace had a fleeting glimpse of the man's profile in silhouette against the shade. It was a profile of an angular, hawk-nosed face that ran down to a pointed angle below the jaw; the profile of a man with a beard. Talbert's profile; the voice had been Talbert's. . . .

Another voice, now; deeper; a little gruff, yet placating: "Yeah. He knew yuh was comin'; that's why he left me here. T' tell yuh. I reckon it'll work out all right. He knowed all yuh was sayin' about it bein' dnagerous, and all. But he figgered that was jest what he wanted. Said all the fightin' men was ridin' the range, so the town'd be empty. . . . He was right disappointed 'bout that haul from the bank. Yuhr tellin' him how much he missed made him crazy t' go back."

"If he hadn't been a fool he'd have made a clean job of it the first time! He should-a known he wasn't gettin' it all, small bills like that! He could'a cleaned the safe then, easy! It was settin' open all the time they was in White's office! And they didn't even look at it! White was laughin' about it, t' me!"

"Aw, yuh can't blame Wes, exactly. He didn't do the collectin' of the money, yuh know. He was holdin' the drop on 'em. The other boys raked in the cash. I reckon they didn't stop t' notice that the stuff in the vault was small bills."

"Damn careless, then! . . . By God, I'm gettin' tired o' the way Wes is runnin' things! What the gang needs is a man with brains enough t' guard against mistakes like that; not just a—killer!"

In the shadow outside the window, Ace Gilbert grinned mirthlessly. Talbert was making a none-too-subtle bid for leadership in place of Luckert! Planting the idea of Luckert's incompetence in the minds of his men . . .

The suggestion did not escape the gruff-voiced one inside. "Meanin' yuh, eh?" The man chuckled. "Yuh got brains all right. This plant here is right neat. But—why don't yuh tell Wes yuh think he's too small for his job? Why don't yuh ask him t' take a back seat and let yuh run things yuhr way a while?"

Talbert's growling answer was inarticulate. The other man laughed shortly and went on. "That's the answer, *sabe?* Yuh ain't man enough t' boss Wes, and yuh ain't man enough t' boss the gang! Reason Wes gets by is, every man in the outfit knows if he crosses the chief he'll get his, and get it quick! He can lick any man o' the lot, guns, firs or foot-racin', and they know it. *I* know it! So I keep my mouth shut!"

Silence for a time, and Gilbert's thought raced unrestrained. Then Talbert's voice again: "Fill it up again, will yuh? I got t' keep awake, somehow! . . . How long's he been gone? How long before he'll be back?"

"Been gone 'bout a half-hour when yuh come in. I reckon he won't hit the Wells before midnight or later, though. He said he was scared o' crossin' the valley; figgered it was bein' watched. So he aimed t' cut straight north into the hills and then swing east and back t' town. Come back the same way, likely, unless he's in a hurry! It'd be daylight, or near that, 'fore he'd get here."

"Hell! I can't wait all night! Some o' my boys may be all right; but there's others I ain't trustin', yet! Hurry them eggs along and I'll ride soon as I finish eatin'. I wish t' God Wes hadn't . . ."

A twig snapped just back of Ace and he whirled, catlike, his hand striking downward to his gun. A man stood at the corner of the house, and Ace saw even as he turned that the man's gun was bared. It was rotten luck! The thought flashed in his mind even as his muscles jerked to complete his draw: rotten luck, to be caught now, just when luck had played into his hand . . .

Something strange about this! Ace halted his draw as the Colt whipped free, his brain slow to take in the thing he saw. The man there at the corner of the house was no more than a black silhouette with the moonlight streaming past him, but it was plain to Ace that there was something wrong. The fellow could have fired before now, certainly. His gun had been leveled when Ace began his draw. But, instead, the man's arms had jerked up crazily—gun-arm, too—and were making funny motions in the air.

And then, suddenly, he knew! The man stepped forward a little so that his figure became clear beyond the corner of the house; and Ace knew, then! The man was fat, and he was making eloquent gestures of peace, and his hat was tipped far back over a round, thick head. It was Martin! Tubby Martin!

"Tubby!" Ace's whisper was very low. "You damned, damned fool! I nearly shot you in two, you idiot! What d'you mean, sneakin' up on me like that?"

Tubby gasped, audibly. "God-a-might, Ace! How'd I know yuh was here? And don'tcha call me a idiot, yuh jackass! It'd been *yuh* that'd got shot if I hadn't recognized yuh just when I did!"

"All right, all right! Get out of here, then! This is no place to start a debate, Tubby! Let's go!"

They circled the house together and made their way out toward the deep arroyo where Ace had left his horse. Ace had led the way there, with Martin following perforce and Tubby was growling: "Now I got t' go back across that yard, damn it! My hoss is on the other side!"

"Never mind that now! How did you get here? Talk fast, Tubby!"

"Smelled that coffee boilin' again! Hell of a time t' be makin' coffee; specially with me sittin' out there hankerin' for some! Came in t' see what was up. Bumped into yuh! Seen yuh start for yuhr gun, and it scared me so I couldn't talk!"

"You didn't hear anybody ridin' out of here a while ago?"

"Didn't hear a thing. Why? Somebody leave?"

"Luckert and his gang left, that's all! But it's nobody's fault, I reckon. They went north, and you were considerably east of north. Maybe my boys further west heard them go. It doesn't matter. You ride from here west around the circle and tell the men to head for town. Meet me in the yard back of Jaxon's livery barn. Be there by midnight if you have to kill your mounts! Send a lighter man with the news after you reach the first pair, *sabe?* I'm goin' on ahead!"

He was in the saddle as he finished, swinging the sorrel toward the east and setting the spurs home. The gelding lunged away, leaving Tubby Martin gasping. It was nine-thirty when Ace looked at his watch within the first mile after that running start. Two hours and a half to midnight. Two hours and a half in which to gather his scattered men and form them to resist a planned attack in town! It would need smart work and hard riding; hard fighting, too, before it was done. Ace wondered vaguely how many men Luckert had taken. Not that that would matter. If all the men Ace had posted on the range arrived in time, they would outnumber Luckert's force, certainly. If not—well, they would fight with what they had!

# 12 · SMOKE OF BATTLE

IT WAS not yet eleven o'clock when Ace reached the Wells, but the town was strangely silent and deserted. Not strangely, perhaps, either. Dave Robertson's posse had been collected from among the men of the Wells and it had not yet returned. Nor were there many men free on the Thunder River range to spend this evening in town. Most of them were riding on one or the other side of a quarrel that would explode into bloody battle when the two opposing factions met.

The sorrel was lathered when Ace drew rein in front of a small white house on the outskirts of the town and left the horse at the street edge. There was no light in the little house but Ace's knock brought a quick challenge, "Who is it?"

"Ace Gilbert, White. Open up!"

The banker came to the door in his nightshirt, bearing a business-like Colt in his hand. "Hello, Ace. Come in." He laid the gun aside as he pulled down the window shades before striking a light. "Thought I recognized your voice, but—no use takin' chances. . . . What's up?"

"This robbery at the bank, White—I understand Luckert's boys missed a fat haul that was in your private safe in your office. That right?"

The banker glanced keenly at his guest. "You ain't aimin' to finish the job, are you, Ace? We've seen one good cowman go bandit in the last few days. Don't tell me you're followin' suit?" It was said banteringly, but there was a vein of seriousness in it, too. Banker White was a man recently burned and still shy!

Ace grinned. "No! But Luckert is! . . . I happened to be on the right spot at the right time tonight to hear about it, *sabe?* Luckert's sore because he missed the big haul, and he's comin' back tonight! . . . Whoa! Wait a minute! You're not goin' out now and spread the news! There's nobody left in this town fit to go against Luckert, you know! I've got plenty of men ridin' this way, now—be here in time to stop the whole thing, I reckon. But just to play safe, I'm advisin' you to sneak down a back alley to the bank and get that money out of the safe! You take care of the money; I'll take care of the bandits! That fair? Then don't let anybody see you go into the bank, and if you do meet anybody, don't talk! If the old men and children in town now tried to stop Luckert, it'd be a massacre! The men I'm bringin' can take care of themselves. That's the difference!

White was already jerking clothing on over his nightshirt, wasting no time in questions or protest. He was nearly ready when Ace finished speaking. "O.K., Ace. I'm takin' your word. You comin' along, or waitin' here?"

"Neither! You get that money and do somethin' with it—I don't care what! Get it out of the bank, I'd say. Then come back here and go to sleep. . . . By the way! Luckert must be aimin' to blow that safe. If there's any papers in it that might be injured or burned, better bring them, too. I might have to wait, you see, for my boys to get here; might have to let him go ahead and blast the safe open. It'll ruin your furniture, maybe; but we can't help that!"

"To hell with the furniture!" White jerked a hat over his tousled hair and followed Ace outside. Hardly more than three minutes had passed since Ace had halted in front of the house before he was in the saddle again; but he had the satisfaction now of knowing that, whether his own plans found failure or success, Luckert's would at least be doomed to disappointment.

There was no sign of life at the livery barn where Ace had appointed his rendezvous and Ace guessed that Jaxon, the owner, had already gone to his bed in the little room at the front which served him as office and home. A few horses moved drowsily about the slatted hay-rick in the yard behind the stable and one whinnied a shrill greeting as Ace halted the sorrel just outside the yard. The hay-rick served as a cover here from the street and there were no houses near. One short block to the south, and on the opposite side of the street, the square bulk of the bank made a black rectangle set apart from the other business buildings of the town by empty lots on either side. Once again Ace wondered how many men Luckert would bring and what plan of attack he would use. It would take time to crack even the ancient safe that stood in White's office. It seemed to Gilbert that two or three men would be better for the job than a larger number; two or three who would slip into the bank through the door at front, or rear, unseen if possible; remain there until the explosion came and then make a concerted dash through the startled town. But it was possible that Luckert might prefer numbers to mobility at a time when any turning in the trail yonder on the range or in the hills might bring him face to face with a strong posse. He hoped that it might be so; that Luckert would ride in at the head of his entire force so that this one coup might end it all. End it, that is, if those other men from Gilbert's vantage points around the range arrived in town in time!

If they did not, Ace wondered if one man could make any showing at all against Luckert's gang. With luck, he might at least down Luckert and one or two; with luck and the advantage of surprise. Though surprise would mean little in such a case. Men engaged in robbing banks *expect* surprise!

The moments seemed interminable. A pedestrian or two clumped down the boardwalks beside the street, homeward bound from poker game or bar. The town was very still. It was the silence that precedes the storm!

The light in White's little home out on the eastern fringe of the town went out as Ace watched, and he knew that the banker had emptied his safe and returned home. That he had gone to bed, as ordered, Ace doubted. That would be expecting almost too much! But he was out of the way.

Fifteen minutes to midnight, Ace stiffened suddenly, staring at the dark hulk yonder that was the bank. A moment ago, its rigid contours had been clean-cut and square against the lighter sky. Now, a mass of more recent shadow broke the vertical line of the rear wall; shadow that moved restlessly like the surface of a murky pool stirred by some inner ferment.

Horses! Ace knew instantly what caused that shadow there; marveled at the perfect stealth that had made their approach unheard. There were the horses on which Luckert's men had come; many horses, judging by the bulk of shadow there; horses left, no doubt, under the guard of a man or two while the rest deployed inside and around the bank.

They were early. Why didn't Tubby and the boys come? How long did it take to blow a safe? Would Cal, or Tubby, or anyone, have the sense to come in quietly,

or would they ride in like charging cavalry to be met
by blasting fire?

He fidgeted uncomfortably in the darkness staring
across the street at the black, mysterious hulk that was
the bank. Once he thought he caught a gleam of light
in a window there, but it was gone instantly and he
was not sure that he had seen aright. A horse in the
corral behind him whinnied shrilly and he felt the cold
shock of the sound strike against his spine. A horse
among those behind the bank answered, but the sound
was choked off almost before it began. The guards yonder were alert! Someone had set hard fingers into the
horse's nose and stopped his neighing with angry force.

"Ace!"

The sibilant whisper rang as loudly in his ears as a
gunshot might have done. Ace whirled, running back
along the corral fence to where the shadow of the hay-
rick made a broad black patch across the ground. Cal
James met him there, and there were other men in the
shadow; mounted men.

"Cal! God, I thought you'd never get here! Luckert's
over there—in the bank! A dozen men or more, looks
like. How many of you?"

"Seven here; more comin'. The boys west of Talbert's
heard Luckert ride out toward the hills and followed
him. The word had already been passed through five of
the posts and Tubby had to ride all the way down to
my hide-out before he caught up!"

"Luckert would lose 'em in the hills, I reckon. That
means there's ten or twelve due here any time; probably
by ones and twos. We can't wait! Cal, take four men
and get around to the back of the bank—quick! Tubby,
take the rest and block the street south of the bank!
They've got just three ways to go when they leave;
south, or east, or north. You two will take 'em if they
go south or east; I'll stay here an stop 'em if they head
north. There'll be more men along before they come, I
reckon, to give me a hand. Hurry, now! They've been
workin' nearly ten minutes in there now!"

The crowd in the shadows behind James split silently

into two parties and deployed as swiftly as trained troops might have done. They had hardly disappeared before Tommy Hitchcock and a JM rider loomed in the moonlight beyond the yard and came down to Ace's side. Ace sent the extra man to join Tubby Martin at the south; kept Hitchcock with him.

"Stay mounted, Tommy," he whispered. "I'll mount when things start. Luckert will come this way, I figure; from the talk I heard, he'll try to get back to the hills, the way he came in. But I had to block every alley, anyway. We may have more men here in time; but whether we do or not, we'll stop 'em! Ride down along the side of the barn, hell-bent, and throw your horse right into 'em. A mix-up like that'll give the rest of the boys a chance to close in. It won't be long, now . . ."

*Boom!*

The muffled thud of the explosion was no more than a single clap of very distant thunder. Someone in Luckert's gang had known how to set his charge and wrap it to kill the noise. Ace mounted swiftly, jerking his gun free as the sorrel fidgeted and turned. In a moment now a dozen desperate men would charge from the shadows behind the bank and gun-lightning would stab the moonlight yonder with veins of fire. Which way would they come?

It seemed an eternity, that moment or two in which no action came. Luckert would be searching the wreckage of that safe now, cursing probably to find it lean of spoils.

"They're movin'!" Hitchcock's whisper broke the tension and Ace found himself suddenly cool and nerveless as the ball began.

"Comin' this way," he said. His voice was low, matter-of-fact. No use whispering now! "Let's go!"

The sorrel quivered under the pressure of Ace's knees. Hitchcock's mount, beside him, reared and fought the bit for a moment. Luckert's men were mounted now; came swinging out into the street, north bound. Ace drove the spurs home and the sorrel lunged down the black lane beside the wall of the barn at reckless speed.

The swift thunder of other hoofs rang in Gilbert's ears and he sensed rather than saw Hitchcock riding close at the sorrel's flank. Out in the street, a man yelled hoarsely and a gunshot split the rolling undertone of pounding hoofs. The fight had begun!

Ace flung an answering shot into the charging mass ahead and yelled a useless order: "Pull up, Luckert! We've got you trapped!" Perhaps Luckert never heard. Ten to one he would not have heeded if he had! The sudden madness of battle was on them all, and in that insanity men do not halt. Guns spat and chattered a fiendish song that turned the night into bedlam. Ace spurred the sorrel again as the horse would have turned to avoid the shock of impact; felt the sodden, smashing weight of the bandits' charge fling his own mount off his feet and down. But even as he fell he knew that the combined shock of his and Hitchcock's charge had done its work! Luckert's riders were hurled before it into yelling, struggling turmoil. The gun-flashes reaching out of the tangle were wild and unaimed. Even Gilbert, falling clear of his maddened horse, remained untouched and clear. He whipped his gun up and fired deliberately at the nearest man; saw him sag and slide down out of the saddle into the mass.

Other guns were firing now; guns from the south and west. Cal James and Martin were spurring into the fight now, and the bandits were fighting more to clear themselves for flight than in any hope of victory.

Ace had a glimpse of a face in the mêlée of struggling men and beasts and he dove toward it, recognizing Hitchcock as the moonlight struck his face. He found Tommy's arm in the crush and hauled him free. A sodden weight descended crushing upon his head as he staggered free, and the world went softly black. Dimly, he heard crashing echoes as the guns kept up their play; heard the muffled drum of plunging hoofs. He even heard Hitchcock's panting thanks: "Thanks, Ace! By God, we stopped 'em!"

And then—darkness. It was only for a moment, but even when his eyes found sight again he had trouble regaining his feet. The blow had left him groggy and he stood swaying drunkenly, reloading his gun by instinct while he sought to focus his wandering gaze. A black shape hurtled past him and he felt a hot blast sear past his cheek as someone fired from the back of a running horse. He shook his head savagely and whipped the cylinder home into his gun; flung it up and hurled a vengeful shot in the direction of those receding hoofs. And then someone caught him in friendly arms and spoke his name.

"Ace! Yuh all right, kid? It's Cal, Cal James! Where yuh hurt?"

"I'm all right! Somethin' hit me on the head. I'm groggy, a little; be all set in a minute. . . . Did they get away?"

Hitchcock's voice, out of the dissolving dark: "He dived into that mess after we charged 'em; pulled me out from under. A horse struck him as we was comin' out."

And Tubby Martin, sane words sandwiched in between pungent oaths: "Get away, hell! Five of 'em'll *never* get away, anywhere! And six'll hang!"

The shadows were clearing now and Ace could make out faces vaguely. "Luckert?" he asked. "What happened to him?"

Martin grunted and turned away a little, moved by emotions too deep even for oaths. "He—he got clear, Ace. It was him that took a shot at yuh as yuh was standin' there re-loadin' yuhr gun. Lucky for him he missed! If he'd got yuh, we'd-a got him! It was fear o' hittin' yuh that kept us from shootin'."

Ace set his jaw grimly and the pain of contracting muscles sent red-hot daggers to his brain. But the pain cleared the mists away somewhat. "Whose chasin' him?" he asked.

Cal James cut in then, apologetically. "We was all afoot, Ace; all but yuh and Tommy. It never occurred t' me that Luckert might go any way but straight at *us;* and I reckon Tubby made the same mistake. When Luckert made his break we had t' go back for horses.

Some o' the boys are after him now. I—I'd've gone, only I wanted t' know if yuh was—all right."

Ace nodded. They were good friends, these men. . . . "They'll never catch him in the dark," he said. "It's all right, though. This breaks up his gang. Cal, take care of the prisoners, will you? Search 'em; put 'em in jail over there; set a guard over 'em. Rest of you boys, hit the hay. You've had enough. . . . Tommy, what happened to the sorrel? Wasn't hurt, was he?"

"Just a bruise or two. Why? Yuh ain't goin' any place, I hope!"

"I'll ride out to the Triangle, that's all. Steve'll be anxious for news. It'll do me good to wear some of the stiffness off before I sleep, *sabe?* No, I'll go alone!" He overrode their protests, climbing stiffly into the saddle even while they tried to dissuade him. "I'll be there in an hour, and I'll do my sleepin' there! . . . So long! It was a good scrap while it lasted, eh, Tommy?"

"It wouldn't've been good for *me* if yuh hadn't done what yuh did, Ace! I'm appreciatin' that."

"Forget it! So long, boys! See you at the dance, to-night!"

Before he had passed the outskirts of the town he met the men who had given chase to Luckert returning emptyhanded and sore. "He give us the slip, Ace. No use tryin' to trail him in the dark."

"It's all right, boys. You go on in and hit the hay. I'll be seein' Robertson in the mornin' and I'll put him on Luckert's trail. I've got a hunch where he'll go. You fellows have done enough."

Once clear of the town, Ace turned the sorrel off the beaten trail again and rode across country at a steady lope. He was not reasoning, now. Ever since the night when he had held Eddy Lane in his arms and watched him die, Ace had been aware of a smouldering, white-hot hate that consumed all other things: a hatred that included Luckert and all his gang. The gang was wiped out, now, and the whole force of his hatred was left to center on one man: Luckert. It was as if that shot that had seared his face as Luckert passed him a while ago had touched the smouldering fires to flame. He acted now on instinct; an unreasoning assurance in his own mind as to what Luckert would do.

He remembered a tale he had heard once of an old colored man who had found a mule after all others had failed. Asked how he had succeeded so well, the old man said: "Pshaw, white folks! Ah jes' 'magined whar I'd go if'n Ah was a mule, and Ah went thar, and thar he be!" Ace was imagining now where he would go if he were Luckert! And the objective in his mind was the Rocking M. Luckert would need a fresh mount, and supplies, before he began the long, hard days of hiding out and he would find both at Talbert's. Likely, too, that the loot of the first attempt at the bank was cached at the Rocking M, and Luckert would want money.

The sorrel's weariness irked Ace immeasureably but he refused to push the horse too much. The sorrel was Steve Cameron's favorite, and he had had a hard day already. Luckert would beat him to the Rocking M, almost certainly. Probably Luckert's mount was comparatively fresh.

Far out across the Thunder River range the sorrel slowed to a walk as he topped a steep incline, and a voice from somewhere jerked Ace out of his revery with a start. "Halt, there! Who's that?" Almost before the first word was clear Ace had whipped his gun up to cover the rocky covert from which the voice had come. It was not Luckert's voice. That certainly withheld his fire. Luckert would have fired first, without warning!

"That depends! You've got the drop, so—who are *you?*"

The man in the ambush grunted. "Yuh, eh, Ace? Didn't recognize yuh on that hoss!" He stood up and Ace recognized him as the moonlight struck his face. It was one of Robertson's posse. "We're camped down yonder a piece. Robertson'll want t' see yuh."

Ace swore, but there seemed no excuse for a refusal. Robertson was sheriff. He should be told of the thing that had happened tonight in town. And, after all, Wes Luckert's capture was a matter of public concern. It occurred to Ace that he had no right to risk Luckert's escape by insisting upon personal revenge. He had been too angry to think of that in town, but now that he had stumbled upon the posse . . .

And so he rode down with the sentry and they roused Robertson to listen to Ace's news. "I'm bettin' he's headin' for the Rockin' M," Ace concluded. "That's where I'm goin', anyway. You can do as you please."

"Still barkin' up that stump, eh?" Robertson chuckled. "I reckon yuh're all wrong, Ace; but we'll tag along, anyway. That's as good a place t' start from as any."

And so it was a posse, more than a dozen strong, that rode at Gilbert's back when they clattered into the ranch-yard at the Rocking M in the early grey of the new dawn. The place seemed empty and deserted, and Ace's ringing knock brought no reply. Robertson laughed. "Talbert and all his boys are out huntin' Luckert already," he said. "There's nobody here."

But Ace had turned the latch and put his shoulder to the door, and as it swung inward the sight revealed inside cut short his reply to Robertson. He stood for an instant, rigid; stepped aside at last and motioned the sheriff to the door. "Look!" he said. "I was right! Luckert's been here, all right—and gone!"

Robertson looked and the mocking laughter in his eyes disappeared suddenly. Jim Talbert lay full length on the floor in there, and his face was turned toward the door: a face from which dead eyes stared sightlessly from below the bloody mass where lead had torn his scalp away. The feeble light from a smoking lamp on a table nearby was enough to show convincingly that the man was dead.

Robertson stepped inside slowly, and as his eyes became accustomed to the light, he saw another figure huddled against a farther wall. Ace entered just behind him, and Robertson pointed. "See who that is!" he said. "Fix that light! I'll tend to Jim."

Ace nodded. The thing was already plain to him; as plain as though he had witnessed it. But he adjusted the lamp and stooped over the figure beside the wall. He had seen the man before: one of the riders Luckert had imported to the Triangle. The man opened his eyes as Ace touched him and Gilbert called to Robertson: "This man's alive!"

Robertson crossed the room quickly and knelt beside Ace. "What happened, Tex?" he said. "Talk, man! Yuh don't want him t' get away after this, do yuh?"

"No! Damn him!" The man's voice was weak and low, but the words were venomously clear. "Wes done it! Luckert! Pulled a boner on that bank job again, and come out here fer his cut o' the first haul! We was dividin' it, aimin' t'—hit the breeze! I reckon he wanted it all, the sonuva——! 'Fore I knowed it, he was shootin'! Downed Talbert, and got me 'fore I had a chance t' draw! I hope —he burns in—hell!"

Robertson stood up. "Get Wilder," he said. "He knows somethin' about doctorin'. We'll leave him here. I'll scatter my men t' cover every trail. We may be in time t' pen him in the valley. He'll have t' go slow, because he don't know where we are and he won't want to run into us! I'm deputizin' yuh, Ace. That suit? Sorry I crossed yuh like I did, before."

"Forget it! Send a man down south of my old brandin' corral and pick up Talbert's riders. They're all right, I reckon. Put one of your men with one of them and they'll be sure t' go straight!"

"Right! Let's ride!"

# 13 • KAY

WITH THE death of his hope of Luckert's capture, Ace felt the full weight of his own weariness descend upon him. Even his mind seemed numbed by it. The long days of constant strain had been worth while, certainly, since they had resulted in the capture of Luckert's men; but just now it seemed to Ace that he had failed. His whole measurement of success depended upon Luckert. Luckert was gone, so all the rest seemed valueless and small. Just now, his one great need was for sleep. Perhaps when he had rested things would seem better.

The sorrel, too, was very tired and Ace let the horse choose his own gait homeward, so that it was mid-morning when they halted at last in the Triangle yard. The wrangler, Tony, came out to take the horse and Ace mumbled a greeting; stumbled wearily up the pathway to the house. Kay met him at the door; flung it open and caught him as he half-staggered toward her.

"What's the matter, Ace?" Her voice was choked with fear for him and the sound of it broke through his weariness a little. He smiled.

"Just tired, imp," he told her. "Let me talk to Steve a minute, and then—I want to sleep! Lord! I'll bet I could sleep a week!"

"Dad isn't here, Ace. He and Ruth and Gordon are in town; rode in early to make preparations for the dance tonight. What's happened?"

He told her, making the story short. "If Steve's in town, he knows most of it by now, anyway," he concluded. "And I'm not aimin' to ride all the way there just to tell him the rest!"

She sprang up, half-supporting him toward the couch in one corner of the main room. "You poor boy," she said. "Lie down now, and sleep! You can nap while I get you something to eat, and then you can go to sleep in earnest! I'll see that no one bothers you. . . ."

He was too tired to protest. She pushed him down upon the couch and adjusted a pillow under his head; moved swiftly about the room, lowering curtains lest the light bother him. He was asleep almost before her tasks were done, and she hovered over him for a moment as a mother hovers about the cradle of her child.

She called him later when she had prepared a meal for him, and he ate hurriedly, still dazed with sleep and half awake. He smiled at her when he had done and stumbled back to the couch; dropped instantly into sound slumber that took no heed of time.

It was late evening when she went to waken him again, and the odors of frying meat and of coffee were drifting once more about the house from the kitchen as Kay tiptoed down the central hall and through the door into the living room. It was very dark there, but the light from the opened door fell through to lend a ghostly radiance across the cot where Gilbert lay. Kay paused for a moment, a little smile curving her lips as she looked at him.

And then she stiffened suddenly, her eyes fixed on another figure that had been lost until now in the shadows against the wall; the figure of a man!

He moved out now, into the clearer light, and she saw that his back was toward her; that he faced and moved toward the sleeping man. Her own approach had been so silent that he had not heard; was not aware even now of her presence in the door. She could not see his face but there was something about the bulk of that shadowy form that seemed to freeze the blood in her veins. The man was Luckert! There was no doubt of it; and, as he passed the window, she saw the moonlight glint on the barrel of a gun he carried in his hand.

If she screamed, awakening Gilbert now, Luckert would fire. Ace would awake to instant alertness, she knew; but he would have no chance to draw in time to meet Luckert's instant shot. The knowledge numbed her senses for a moment. Luckert had paused now at the foot of the couch and she heard him chuckle softly as he made sure as to who was there. The sound chilled her nerves; brought an icy, desperate calm. She moved out of the doorway with swift, sure steps that made no sound; crept past the door through which Luckert had come and sought the darkness of the wall, as he had done.

She reached the window at last, and Luckert's back loomed before her not two yards away. He was lifting his gun now and she saw it steady as he made certain of his aim.

"Gilbert!"

Luckert's husky whisper startled Kay and her sudden movement almost betrayed her. Luckert glanced around but the girl was hidden still in the shadows and he did not see.

"Gilbert!" His whisper was louder now and Ace stirred restlessly. "Wake up, damn yuh! . . . That's better! Thought I'd pulled out, didn't yuh? Not till I've finished *yuh,* I won't! I thought I'd lost yuh; had t' come here anyway after the money I've cached here—and here yuh are! That's luck, eh? Luck for me! I'm goin' to kill yuh, Gilbert! I said I would, and by God . . ."

Kay's nerves broke under the strain of waiting, and she screamed Gilbert's name. Luckert whirled and as he turned Kay sprang at him like a maddened cat, clutching at the arm that swung the gun. There was a spurt of flame and a roar as Luckert fired, but Kay's act had deflected his aim and the shot crashed into the wall over Gilbert's head. A flailing sweep of Luckert's arm hurled the girl heavily against the wall and broke, momentarily, her frenzied clutch. The gun whipped back toward Gilbert, fired as it moved, and the heavy slug ripped the couch where Ace's body had lain less than a second before. But even as he fired Luckert must have realized his mistake.

Gilbert had flung himself sideways as Kay screamed,

twisting his body off the couch onto the floor. His hands groped wildly for his guns which he had dropped, with his hat and spurs, beside the couch before he fell asleep. But before his fingers felt the leather of the holsters Luckert's gun whipped down once more, fire burst from the muzzle, and Ace was stunned by the terrific impact of the lead that tore through his left shoulder high up by his neck. The thought flashed through his mind that the next shot would finish him. But that shot never came.

A veritable fighting fury, Kay was on her feet again. Both her hands seized Luckert's arm and she sank her teeth into the man's flesh. Luckert swore at the sharp pain, found he could not lift his gun, and stepped to the door, pulling the girl between himself and Gilbert.

Ace reached his guns and leapt to his knees, only to find that he would hit Kay if he shot. Luckert, still holding Kay before him, stepped backward into the hall and kicked the door shut just as Ace jumped forward in a vain effort to reach him with his hands. He thrust Kay heavily against the door and called loudly, "Shoot through the door, Gilbert, and yuh'll kill the gal! And if yuh try to come through it I'll kill her myself!"

With a savage wrench he broke Kay's grip and before she could scream he brought the barrel of his gun down on her head with a sickening thud. Kay's body went limp and Luckert let her slide to the floor against the door. Turning, he ran down the hall and out of the house.

His horse was tethered to a tree a hundred yards away. As Luckert made for the spot, he saw the wrangler, Tony, awakened by the gunplay, coming at a dead run from the bunkhouse, a gun swinging from each hand. Quickly Luckert wheeled and shot, but though the moonlight was very bright the distance was too great and Tony came on, firing as he ran. Luckert fired again, this time more carefully, and Tony stopped in his tracks, wavered, and sank to the ground. Luckert reached his horse and flung himself into the saddle. Lifting the animal's forelegs high into the air, Luckert whirled him around and galloped down the drive, through the gateway, turned sharply to the right, and headed for the mountains in the distance. There, he knew, he could elude pursuit.

And Luckert was afraid. His last glimpse of Ace, wounded though he was, had shown him the almost maniacal fury in the man's eyes. A cold chill of the fear of death had trickled into him and broken, for the time, his bullying courage. The cold blue peaks of the mountains, outlined sharply in the moonlight, spelled the only safety now.

Ace had stopped short at Luckert's threat to Kay. The man was brute enough to shoot her to save his own skin, and Ace felt he must act carefully. Quickly he turned, strapping on his gunbelt, crossed the room, and quietly opened a window which faced toward the back of the house. Not without difficulty he climbed through the opening and dropped onto the grass outside. His left arm, he found, was helpless. He couldn't lift it, and sharp, burning pains were beginning to shoot through his shoulder. He could feel the hot blood running down.

Shots from the other side of the house suddenly assailed his ears, and he froze in desperate anxiety. Had Luckert carried out his threat? Had he killed the girl? Ace instantly came to life. Forgetting his pain and his crippled condition, he rushed 'round the house toward the door, a gun ready in his right hand. Hoofbeats reached his ears, and he saw Luckert, just as the latter left the trail and cut out onto the range.

Ace tore into the house and dropped to his knees beside the still form of the girl against the living room door. Half lifting, half dragging her, he got her into the living room and laid her on the couch from which he had just now so narrowly escaped. He knelt beside her, calling her name, and searched in vain for indications of a wound.

"Kay . . . Kay, honey, speak to me!" God! If Kay were dying then death would be too merciful for Luckert! Ace lifted her body, cradling it almost roughly in his arm. "Kay, darlin'! It's Ace, Kay! Say you're all right, won't you, Kay?"

She stirred weakly, spoke to him sleepily. "What's—what's happened, Ace?" And then, as fuller consciousness returned "Luckert! You—he—he didn't get you, Ace? . . . Oh, God, I'm glad. . . ."

She closed her eyes. His arm gave way suddenly and she fell back upon the couch. "Kay . . . honey . . . I—I thought *you* were dead, too, for a minute! You're not wounded? He didn't hurt you?"

"No," the girl whispered. "He didn't shoot me. I'm all right. He hit me on the head. I—I guess I fainted. But, Ace!" She caught at him with both her hands. "Luckert! Where is he? You haven't told me!"

Ace's voice grew firm and cold as he spoke. "He got away, Kay, darlin'," he said. "And I'm going after him." He got to his feet. "You lie there and rest, honey. When it's over I'll be back. Luckert has gone too far this time!"

Kay sat bolt upright. "No! No!" she cried. "Ace! you mustn't go! You might be hurt!"

"You know I've got to go, honey, and the sooner the better."

And before she could protest, Ace stooped and closed her lips with a kiss that carried her back to the day when she stepped off the train to be greeted by just such an unbrotherly embrace.

Ace moved fast. At a dead run he made for the corral. He threw open the bars, stepped inside. The horses, only a few of them left, were bunched at the far end.

"Satan! Here!" he called, and whistled low and sharp. There was a movement among the animals and presently, with a whinny for greeting, the big white stallion detached himself from the group and approached his master. Ace dragged a saddle from the rail and threw it over the lean back. Working as fast as his one good arm would let him, he strapped the saddle and secured the bridle. "Can't play safe with you this time, Satan," he told the horse as he worked. "You've got to see me through, old boy!"

The horse seemed to understand and no sooner was Ace firmly seated in the saddle than he was off down the

driveway at a fast pace. Ace pulled him off the trail at
the spot where Luckert had left it, leaning low over the
splendid neck as he touched his heels sharply to the
animal's flanks. A tremendous burst of speed answered
the touch, the steady, rhythmic gallop of a great thoroughbred eating up the miles.

The cold night air whistled past Ace's ears and cooled
the aching throb in his wounded shoulder. He began to
wonder what Luckert would be up to. "Likely cut
straight across the range to the hill country," thought
Ace. "He'll lay low till daylight, then find a trail up-
country and won't stop till he's on the other side. That
is—unless I catch him first!" He smiled grimly. Luckert's
horse would be no match for Satan.

An hour passed, during which the steady speed of the
white horse never slackened. The mountains were now
so close that they seemed to loom high over Ace's head.
Within a few minutes, he knew, the moon would drop
behind them and darkness would end the pursuit for
the night.

But at that moment, not very far ahead, he detected a
movement, vague and yet distinct to his keen eyes. He
bent lower in the saddle, struck almost savagely at the
horse with his heels, and was rewarded with an extra
burst of speed. Five minutes passed and he saw it again,
much nearer. It was a man on a horse, traveling at a gallop! A few seconds later the thunder of Satan's hoofs
must have reached the man ahead because he turned in
the saddle and looked back, swerving his mount vio-
lently to one side as he did so. Satan was gaining fast,
and before the man faced forward again, Ace knew that it
was Luckert! The outlaw spurred his horse furiously,
but the animal, tired from the many miles covered before this mad dash across the range began, failed to re-
spond. Satan on the other hand, seeming to sense his
master's objective close at hand, put forth his tremendous
reserve power and the gap between the pair closed
rapidly.

Luckert turned in the saddle again and from the semi-
darkness ahead Ace saw several rapid bursts of flame.

But Luckert couldn't hit, riding at that speed; his bullets passed wide of their mark.

Ace dropped his reins altogether and brought his gun from the holster at his side. But instead of firing he waited grimly as the distance between them continued to close.

Suddenly, as if in desperation, Luckert brought his horse to a sudden halt, throwing the animal into the air. He leaped from the saddle, faced about, and emptied his revolver at his pursuer. But fear and the strain of the long hours must have spoiled One-shot Farley's famous aim. The lead sang close about Ace's ears, but again none found its mark. Luckert was reloading furiously.

Then, not having fired a shot, Ace hauled Satan up short, and threw himself bodily to the ground, keeping his feet with great dexterity. The two men faced each other, barely twenty yards apart. Both guns came up together.

But Ace was a fraction of a second ahead of his opponent. There was a flash as he fired from the hip, five more as he gradually raised the gun to eye level.

Luckert squeezed out one shot, his body crumpling simultaneously. He managed to fire again, wildly, but the stream of lead from Ace's gun had told its tale with accuracy. While Ace was firing, the impact of the shots seemed almost to be holding Luckert on his feet; when he suddenly ceased, Luckert collapsed like a burst balloon, and Ace knew that each of his shots had met its mark.

And just at the moment when the dead body of the outlaw fell with its face in the sandy ground, the moon, as if alarmed at the sight, passed out of sight behind the mountains, and heavy darkness, like a funeral pall, closed in on the lonely range.

Kay was up and about and had changed into a gay party dress when Ace wearily opened the ranch-house door, entered the living-room and dropped to the couch. The strain of the last two hours, together with his loss of blood, had told on him and his body felt too tired to move.

"Ace!" she cried as she came into the room. "Dear! Are you all right?" Then, as her eyes took in his blood-stained shirt, she gave a little scream and rushed to him. "You're hurt! Oh, Ace, you shouldn't have gone! I asked you not to!"

Hurriedly she left the room, to return at once with bandages and a basin of hot water. Ace bared his shoulder and tenderly she bathed the wound, bandaged it securely, made a sling for the helpless arm. Somehow, Ace noticed it no longer hurt him. Kay's concern made him feel almost grateful for it.

She brought him a fresh, clean shirt. "It's Dad's," she said simply, "but it will fit you."

When he had changed she took him in her arms and he buried his face in her fragrant hair. As he told her, the horror of it all came back to him with a rush. Holding her tight, he pushed her a little distance away. She felt his body shaken for a moment with racking sobs as she gazed at him through tear-filled eyes.

"Luckert's dead, honey," he choked. "And I thought he'd killed you, Kay. I can't ever forget that, darlin'. Are you sure you're all right?"

She smiled suddenly through her tears and once more held him to her. "I'm all right, Ace . . . I'm all right! . . . Did you—care so much, my dear?"

It was over soon. Ace pulled away from her arms at last and stood up, lifting her with him. He laughed a little, brokenly. "I'm—sorry, Kay. Actin' like a—fool kid . . . You—saved my life, imp; and then for a minute I thought you a goner yourself! I—I never went soft like that before . . . I don't know why . . ."

But *she* knew; and he knew, too! He turned away from her, refusing to meet her eyes. He loved her! He loved Kay—not Ruth! God! What a mess it all was! It must have been Kay, all along! He remembered now how sweet her lips had been when she had kissed him that day at the station. And even after that he had still thought he cared for Ruth! What a fool he had been! He had never loved Ruth as he loved Kay now; had never felt the fierce, consuming hunger for her that was on him now. It had taken the sudden shock that had come tonight to reveal the truth, but it was clear now! Too clear! Too clear because it was hopeless. He realized that, too; that he could not break his word to Ruth! Ruth had been loyal to him; had remained loyal even when she might have taken a man like Wallace. She must have loved him to reject Wallace for him. It would be damnable to turn traitor to her now!

Tony, his head wrapped in a bandage, came up from the barn then, and Ace told the wrangler of Luckert's death. Tony told of his own shooting affair, protesting that he was not badly hurt; that the force of Luckert's bullet had stunned him for only a few moments, inflicting only a scalp wound as it passed him. He'd ride into town and have the doc look at it.

"Saddle a horse for me before you go, will you, Tony?" Kay added the request as Tony turned to go. "And you might saddle one for Ace, too. Satan's had enough for one night. I may be able to persuade him to take me to the dance, even if it is getting late!"

Later still, Ace ate the supper that Kay had prepared for him. It was odd, he thought, how life went on in its accustomed rut even after the world had exploded for a man! Even Kay seemed not to notice any change! Just the same sweet, sisterly kid she had always been, taking care of him as she had always done. . . .

"Sure, I'll take you to the dance, Kay," he told her. "I don't look very dressed up, I reckon; and it's too far from home to change; but—I'll take you."

It was a silent ride in to town. Kay talked at first, cheerfully trying to coax her escort out of his almost surly mood. But she failed and so she fell silent, too, watching him thoughtfully as she rode beside him, longing to help him in the fight she knew he was making, yet fearful to intrude. There was nothing she could say, after all, that would not be disloyal either to herself or

Ruth. She knew what his trouble was; knew that he loved her; understood that he had discovered his love in that awful moment when he had thought her dead. But knowing made no difference. It was for him to decide.

There was a light in a window above the General Store where they tied their mounts and Kay pointed it out laughingly. "Poker game," she diagnosed. "Women folks all gone to the dance, so the Big Six are at it again!"

Ace nodded. "Only it's the Big Five, I reckon, tonight. Robertson's out of it. The rest of the county office-holders are up there, though. They'll miss Dave, too. He's the consistent loser!"

Kay laughed softly. "Remember when that horse wrangler from up north eloped with Samuelson's girl? Brought her to the Wells and broke into the poker game up there and made the clerk issue a license and got the judge to marry them? There's an idea for you, Ace! What your love-making needs, as I told you before, is a little enthusiasm! Why not kidnap Ruth tonight and yank her over here before she can yell for help?" It was a silly thing to say; almost like taunting him with his trouble. But it was out now!

He stood stiffly for a moment, silent. "Not a bad idea," he said, at last. "Get it over with!" He did not guess that she understood; that she knew that he was considering her suggestion as good in the light of an irrevocable step from which, once taken, he could not draw back. Perhaps it *was* a good idea! Perhaps it would be best to rush into a marriage with Ruth before some chance word or look betrayed his love for Kay, and spoiled everything for all of them!

They went across the street then, into the lighted corridor from which stairs climbed to the dance hall on the second floor. He lost Kay almost at once when they reached the crowd, surrendering her after one short dance to an eager group of swains. Steve Cameron reached him then and Ace drew him aside to tell him of Luckert's death.

"I reckon I ought to say I'm sorry, or somethin' like that, Steve; him bein' your brother, and all that. But . . ."

"Yuh needn't, Ace. I—owe yuh a debt o' gratitude for what yuh've done, as a matter o' fact. I'm sorry he was—what he was; but I'm not sorry he's dead. I can't be! . . . Nobody here knows, even, that he was my brother! Seems funny, doesn't it? I'll see Robertson to-morrow—tell him . . ."

"I've been thinkin' about that." Ace laid a hand on Cameron's arm. "Nobody knows about that, Steve, except me and Wallace and O'Keefe. Wallace is leavin'. Tim'll never tell, and I won't. What's the use of lettin' anybody else know? It can't do any good, and it might do you a lot of harm."

"Kay knows."

Ace laughed shortly. "You know Kay'd never tell, Steve! Be sensible!"

There was more talk, Ace urging and Cameron loath to yield in spite of his real desire. But Cameron compromised at last, and they left it so: "We'll put it up to Robertson, Ace. Dave's a white man, and he represents the law. We'll tell him, and if he says to keep it secret, fine! It'd mean a lot t' me, bein' able to go on with my work."

The dance was a mockery to Ace. He danced with Ruth; surrendered her in a little while to Wallace. He danced with Kay; found the precious contact with her a torture. And so he left the hall after a little while, stalking out into the dark to be alone.

Others had sought the open, too; couples strolling beneath the summer moon. From the shadow of a nearby store Ace watched them pass him, hearing the low murmur of their voices and sometimes the music of a woman's laughter.

A couple sauntered down toward him from the dance hall, their heads close together as they talked in murmuring undertones. They halted where the shadow of the store reached out across the sidewalk and Ace saw the girl turn suddenly and put out her arms. The man caught her hungrily; held her tight in a long embrace. They were so near now that Ace could not move without being seen, and so he waited in the darkness for them to go on. Their voices came to him presently, low but very clear.

"Oh, I love you so much, my dear! It's too beautiful to be spoiled like this! And yet—I can't tell him! You see that, don't you? It wouldn't be—fair!"

Ace stiffened suddenly, doubting his ears. The voice was Ruth's! And the man—he was speaking now and there was no mistaking those clipped, terse sentences. It was Wallace!

"Oh, quite! Trusts you, Gilbert does. Has a perfect right to, of course. Mustn't hurt him. Loyalty. All that sort of thing. You're loyal, and I—I love you for it. But it hurts!"

They were gone after a while. It seemed to Ace that he must have stood there for hours, seeking sanity amid the turmoil of his thoughts. The fact was, then, that Ruth loved Wallace! She had rejected Wallace out of loyalty to Ace! Why, that was the reason he had not declared his love for Kay—loyalty! Loyalty to Ruth! He laughed suddenly, loud and clear. He and Ruth, breaking their hearts out of loyalty to each other! Why, they might have gone on, ruining four lives out of a mistaken sense of duty! But not now!

He forgot his weariness; forgot the foul mood that had been upon him; ran back toward the brilliant hall, still laughing softly to himself. The hall was empty and he ran through it to the foot of the stairs leading up to the crowded hall. Ruth and Wallace were standing on the landing just above him and as Ace began the ascent Ruth turned toward him and started down.

"I've been looking for you, Asher." Wallace had turned away into the crowd and the two on the stairs stood alone. "I—I want you to—marry me, Asher! Tonight! Kay—said something about the poker game somewhere—the county clerk, and a judge . . . We could get married there. I—don't want to wait any more, Asher."

His laughter died suddenly. A cold fear clutched him; fear that what he had seen and heard out there a while ago had been a dream! But then he understood. Once more he started to speak but Ruth was quicker. Her voice was a bit too high now, and there were unshed tears in her eyes. She tried to mask them with laughter but the laughter was forced and false.

"Better—take me quickly, Asher! I—I might change my mind and make you—wait again! I . . . Oh, don't ever say I didn't play fair, at least! I'm trying to!"

That last sentence, at least, rang true! Ace *knew* then; knew that he had seen and heard aright out there beneath the moon! Ruth was throwing herself at him now to save herself from disloyalty she might regret, just as he had thought a while ago of kidnapping her lest he declare his love to Kay!

"Why . . . why, sure, dear! That's—that's great! I . . . Look, Ruth, you go down to the foot of the stairs and wait for me in the hall, will you? I—I'll need some money; get it—upstairs. You wait for me, will you? It'll only be a minute."

She nodded; turned from him blindly and went down the stairs. Gordon Wallace had mingled with the crowd above so that it took a minute or two for Ace to find him, but when he did he dragged the startled man to the stairs and held him while he talked.

"I never knew it till tonight, *amigo,* but there's such a thing as bein' *too* square! And you're it! You see, I heard what Ruth said to you down there by the store a while ago; and it's all right, understand? It's *all right!* She's waitin' for you down at the foot of the stairs now, see? She thinks it's me she's waitin' for, but she'll be glad to see you! You tell her I sent you! Tell her—tell her the idea about visitin' the poker game across the street is a good one, understand? Remember now! Poker game—across the street! Tell her that!"

But Wallace was gasping; refused to be hurried. "Oh,

I say, Gilbert! That business down by the store—It was unintentional, you know! Emotional outburst, all that! She didn't mean it, you know! I won't . . ."

Ace whirled him about to face the stairs. "Don't argue, damn it!" he said, joyously. *"It's all right,* I tell you! I found out tonight that I'm in love with Kay, understand? *Kay,* not Ruth! I was breakin' my heart because I couldn't tell Ruth about it after the way she'd stuck to me! Now, beat it, will you? Ruth's waitin' for you! And—congratulations!"

It took a moment for the truth to sink in, but Gordon Wallace rallied gamely after a while! "By George, Gilbert! That's great! Perfectly ripping! She loves you, you know! Splendid girl! Glad she's getting what she wants, by George I am! . . . Glad for me, too! Decent of you! Sorry; got to go now . . ."

Ace watched him go, fairly stumbling down the stairs in his eagerness. He disappeared around the railing at the foot of the stairs and Ace tiptoed down part way to lean out across the banister to watch. What he saw must have pleased him, for he was laughing aloud when he turned to climb the stairs again. Turned—to face Kay Cameron, on the landing looking down!

"What in the world are you doing, Ace? Are you drunk, or—what? I thought at first you were going to slide down the banister, but you must have thought better of it! . . . What are you laughing at?"

He took the steps at a bound; caught both her hands in his. "You said once that you'd want the man you loved to bully you—and humor you—and flatter you by bein' an utter fool about you! Is that still right?"

She nodded, wide-eyed. "Yes! But what . . ."

"Shut up!" He bent low, scooping her up in his arms. "I've been a fool about you all your life," he said; "and now I'm bullying you! And I'll keep on doin' it till you say you love me, Kay! Because *I* love *you!* And if we hurry, Kay, we can catch Ruth and Wallace in time to make it a double wedding!"

They were down the stairs now and the hallway was

still deserted. He halted there, briefly. "It's all right, isn't it, Kay? You—you do—love me, don't you?"

Her answer was inaudible, but it must have been a satisfactory one to Ace; for his laughter rang in tune with hers as they ran like boisterous children toward the doorway of the general store across the street!